Deceitful Death

Gerald Hinton's eve-of-wedding stag party at the London Arts and Letters Club was interrupted by a glamorous 'Golden Girl' whom Gerald claimed never to have seen before. But the girl declared herself pregnant and named Gerald as the father of her child. True or false? A hoax in bad taste or a serious attempt to prevent the wedding? No one knew—Gerald least of all. But there was nothing of a hoax about the two deaths that followed; they were all too distressingly real.

John Breland, Harley Street doctor, was both a guest at the party and a member of the club. His friendship with Gerald soon involved him in efforts to solve the mysteries, and in a volatile relationship with Chief Superintendent Freeman of Scotland Yard.

JOHN PENN

Deceitful Death

COLLINS, 8 GRAFTON STREET, LONDON W1

William Collins Sons & Co. Ltd
London · Glasgow · Sydney · Auckland
Toronto · Johannesburg

This book is fiction. All the characters and incidents in it are entirely imaginary.

First published 1983
© John Penn 1983

British Library Cataloguing in Publication Data

Penn, John
Deceitful Death. — (Crime Club).
I. Title
823′.914[F]   PR6066.E/

ISBN 0 00 231363 4

Photoset in Compugraphic Baskerville
Printed in Great Britain by
T. J. Press (Padstow) Ltd

CHAPTER 1

John Martin Breland said goodbye to his patient on the landing. He returned to his first-floor consulting room and crossed to the elegant long windows, watching for a moment the never-ceasing struggle for taxis that was such a feature of Harley Street life. On this dull June morning each side of the narrow road was a forest of arms and umbrellas, waving among the parked cars.

Dr Breland glanced at his watch. Good! He was running early. Normally he saw patients at half-hourly intervals — twenty or twenty-five minutes for consultation and examination, and five or ten to write up his case notes and compose himself. Private Harley Street medicine was very satisfying, he told himself. There weren't many such general practices left in central London, especially in this part of Marylebone traditionally devoted to consultants and specialists and clinics. He was glad that four years ago he'd heard of this vacancy and, thanks to the generosity of an aunt, had been able to raise the money to buy into it.

At first he'd had doubts. Unlike his father's practice in Devon that he'd joined as soon as he'd qualified, this was medicine for the rich, the near-rich and the heavily-insured. He'd felt some guilt about deserting the National Health Service, but had come to realize he was serving a real need. Maybe one day he would return to ordinary general practice, perhaps even rejoin his father, but not yet. For the present, Brel was happy here in London, living in the flat that went with the partnership, at the top of this Harley Street house.

Kathleen Taylor, his nurse and secretary, came through from her small adjoining office. Dr Breland, his thoughts interrupted, returned to his desk and made a note on his last patient's file before putting it aside. With her usual efficiency, Kathleen rearranged the examination couch behind the screen, made sure that a clean uncrumpled gown was ready for the next patient, checked that everything was in place.

She said, 'Brel —'

'What?'

'Mrs Carling's cancelled her appointment this afternoon.'

'At the last moment again? Damn the woman! It's the third or fourth time she's done it. She seems to think we're just here for her convenience. I've a good mind to send her a bill.'

Smiling, Kathleen shook her head. 'No need. I was able to fit another patient into her slot — a Miss Sally-Ann Belmont. You've not seen her before. I told her you liked to have an hour with new patients, but she insisted and in the circumstances —'

'Great. That's all right. Did she say what she wanted?'

'She's four months pregnant, and she's worried about abdominal pain.'

Brel lifted his dark head and gave his secretary his full attention. 'You told her I wasn't in the business of quickie abortions, especially at that stage?'

'Don't be so suspicious, Brel. The question didn't arise. The poor girl's afraid something may be going wrong.'

'Then why come to me? She must have seen another doctor by this time.'

'She explained all that on the phone. She lives in Cornwall. She's only in London for a few days on holiday, and she's no intention of going to a hospital casualty department.'

'But why me? Did she stick a pin in the phone book?'

'No, no. She was given your name by a friend of yours — Gerald Hinton.'

'Ah! I see. Why didn't you say so in the first place?'

'You didn't give me a chance.'

Brel grinned, causing a deep cleft to appear in each cheek of his attractive face. His informal though professional relationship with Kathleen Taylor — happily married and more than ten years older than he was — had been firmly established very soon after he had taken over the practice. 'Okay, Kathleen, you win. Now it's time for the next customer.'

As Kathleen returned to her office to signal the receptionist on the ground floor to send up the last patient before lunch, Dr Breland rose to his feet and went towards the door to welcome him. Brel was tall — just over six feet — and in his early thirties. Many of his patients — especially the younger women — wondered why he wasn't already married. The truth was quite simple. So far he'd been happy enough with girl-friends. Marriage was for the future.

Miss Belmont's appointment was for three o'clock, and at precisely that time she was shown into the consulting room, bringing with her a waft of expensive perfume. She was tall and athletic-looking and moved with the studied grace of a model or dancer. Her clothes, including a mink stole that was scarcely justified by the warmth of the June day, matched the quality of her scent. Seated across the desk from Brel she regarded him with big blue eyes, and gave him what could only be described as a dazzling smile.

'It's terribly good of you to see me at such short notice, Doctor.' Her voice was low, husky, well-modulated.

'Not at all, Miss Belmont. Any friend of Gerald Hinton —'

'Oh yes, Gerry. He's a wonderful guy, isn't he?' Somehow her words sounded forced or insincere.

'You've known him some time?' asked Brel.

'Well, a little while. I met him casually and we got on well together.'

The blue eyes were cast down, and Brel was able to study the heart-shaped face, impeccably made-up, and the head of carefully-styled bronze-coloured hair. Clearly Miss Belmont devoted much time and money to her appearance. The result was very attractive, but Brel was not unduly impressed. He preferred his girls to be altogether more natural.

'Now, Miss Belmont, I'd like to know something about you,' he said briskly. 'Then we can discuss your condition, and perhaps I can examine you.' He pulled a pad of paper towards him. 'First, your full name and address and phone number, please.'

'Sally-Ann Belmont and I live in deepest Cornwall. Do you know Cornwall, Doctor?'

'Not very well.'

Brel waited. Miss Belmont produced the information, and he wondered what such a hot-house flower did with herself in the depths of the country. Possibly he'd misjudged her. She might be equally at home standing, wind-blown, at the edge of a cliff, striding across the moors or galloping a favourite horse along the sands.

He said abruptly, 'Age?'

'Twenty-six.'

Mentally adding three or four years, Brel wrote down 'Twenty-six plus'. 'Have you ever had any serious illnesses? Any operations?'

'No. Just the usual things when I was a child. I'm disgustingly healthy.'

'Abortions?' It was a throwaway word.

Sally-Ann Belmont laughed. 'Not me. I've always been too careful.'

The laugh and the words jarred on Brel, but he merely smiled professionally. 'And your usual general practitioner, Miss Belmont? I need your doctor's name and address, so that I can write to him.'

'Why on earth would you want to do that?' The big blue eyes were suddenly wary.

'It's customary in circumstances like these. After all —'

'What a lot of nonsense! I can tell him what you say.'

'Please, Miss Belmont.'

'Oh, all right! But he's only seen me once, just to confirm I was pregnant.'

'Surely he mentioned the need for regular check-ups?'

'Oh yes. He said I should see him at intervals, but I haven't. I told you, till now I've been disgustingly healthy. Normally I never go near a doctor.'

Brel waited, making no response, and with an irritated shrug Miss Belmont gave him her GP's name and address. 'Any more questions?' she asked sharply.

'Only about these pains you've been having, Miss Belmont,' said Brel. 'Tell me —' She answered his questions with some hesitation, but quite clearly. An intelligent patient, he thought. Finally, he said, 'I should like to examine you. Would you undress and get on the couch. There's a gown hanging behind the screen. And there's a bell on the little table. Just ring it when you're ready.'

With an encouraging nod to his new patient, the doctor stood up, pushed back his chair and went into the adjoining office where Kathleen was busy typing. Her fingers continuing to move over the keys, she looked up. 'You want me?'

'Please. She's quite a dish, and she's a bit odd.' Brel paused. 'I mean it, Kathleen. I can't put my finger on it, but there's something about her that —' He broke off as the bell rang. 'She's been quick.'

In the consulting room Sally-Ann Belmont was ready for them. She had undressed and was lying on her back on the examination couch. She had slipped into the gown, but had not bothered to draw it about her, so that her body was exposed, the full breasts, the bush of gingery hair, the long slim legs—and the thickening waist. Without the disguise of clothes it was quite evident that Miss Belmont was pregnant.

Kathleen Taylor went forward quickly and pulled the gown around the patient, and Dr Breland examined her with care. He could find nothing wrong. She seemed to be, as she said, a healthy, strong young woman. There was nothing immediately apparent to account for the somewhat nebulous pains of which she complained. It crossed Brel's mind that perhaps she really was in search of an abortion. But why leave it so late, and why come here? It wasn't something for which Gerald would have recommended him.

At length he said. 'That's fine. Thank you, Miss Belmont. You can get dressed now.'

Kathleen went back to her office, carefully leaving the interconnecting door open, and Brel sat down at his desk. He made some notes. He was a good doctor, and conscientious. Miss Belmont puzzled him. There could be plenty of organic explanations for her pains, some trivial and some serious, but on the other hand her symptoms could be entirely functional or even psychosomatic. Without tests it was impossible to be sure.

He was still considering the problem when Sally-Ann Belmont appeared from behind the screen. She had dressed as quickly as she had undressed, but looked immaculate. Brel rose and waved her to the chair in front of him. The door to Kathleen's office was quietly closed.

'How long are you staying in London, Miss Belmont?'

'I haven't decided. Why do you ask, Doctor?'

'Because I can find nothing wrong with you, nothing to account for the discomfort you've been having. But the sort of examination I can give you here can't rule out everything. So, if you're staying in London, I would suggest you see a consultant gynaecologist. It can easily be arranged, and he might want to admit you to a clinic for a night or two. Otherwise —'

'No. That won't be necessary. Thanks all the same.' Miss Belmont uncrossed her long legs and stood up. 'It was probably just indigestion. But I'm very grateful to you for seeing me, Doctor, very grateful.' She was surprisingly effusive.

'As you wish. But you must consult your own doctor when you get home. I'll be dropping him a line. There's no point in taking risks with the baby at this stage, is there?' Brel also rose to his feet. 'I hope all goes well in the next few months, Miss Belmont,' he added.

'Thanks. I intend it shall.' She opened her handbag. 'If I could settle with you now, Doctor.'

'Miss Taylor will see to that.' Brel had pressed the bell under his desk, and Kathleen was already in the room. He held out his hand. 'Goodbye, Miss Belmont.'

'Goodbye, Doctor. Though I shouldn't be surprised if we met again.' The thought seemed to amuse her.

'Of course, if you have any more trouble while you're in London.' He paused as a thought struck him. 'Or do you mean at the wedding?'

'Wedding? What wedding is that?'

'I meant Gerald Hinton's wedding — to Elizabeth Lydney.'

'Elizabeth Lydney?' Tiny frown marks appeared between the blue eyes.

'Yes. Gerald and Elizabeth are getting married at the end of the month. Surely you —'

'Oh yes. I had heard about it, of course. But I've not been invited, so we shan't be meeting there, Doctor.'

With a casual wave Miss Belmont followed Kathleen into the next office. As the door closed behind them Brel shook his head in puzzlement. He wondered . . .

Minutes later Kathleen came back into the consulting

room. She found Brel pouring over a copy of the Medical
Directory.

'She's gone?'

'Miss Belmont? Yes. But don't worry, she paid her bill.'

'I hope it wasn't with a dud cheque.' Brel sounded
grim.

'Cash, actually.' Kathleen was mildly surprised. She
had spoken in jest. It was unlike Brel to be anxious about
a fee. 'Why would you expect a cheque of hers to bounce?'

'Because she's a phoney, or I strongly suspect so. I had
to press her for the name of her GP, and she produced
one that doesn't exist.'

'Are you sure?'

Brel looked at the date on the book in front of him.
'Yes, I'm sure. Unless he's qualified in the last couple of
years and started a country practice in Cornwall.' Brel
glanced at his watch. 'Look, I've not got time now. I don't
want to keep Mrs Anderson waiting. But as soon as you've
shown her in, check with the latest Directory, will you,
and check Miss Belmont's supposed home phone number.
Here's her file.'

'Okay, if you think it matters.'

'It probably doesn't, but—' Brel shrugged. 'I don't
know. I dislike patients who deliberately deceive me. Why
should she bother to lie?'

'Maybe no one where she lives knows she's pregnant,
and she doesn't want you breaking the glad news to the
local doctor.'

'Well, if they don't know now, they damn soon will.'
Brel was impatient. 'Anyway, see what you can do.'

'All right,' replied Kathleen.

Mrs Anderson liked to talk, and her appointment ran
well over the half-hour. Then there was a long phone call
from his senior partner. Inevitably Brel got more and
more behind, and it was after six when, with a sigh of
relief, he said goodbye to his last patient of the day. He

had all but forgotten about Miss Sally-Ann Belmont.

'Sorry to have kept you so late, Kathleen.'

'That's okay. I wasn't doing anything tonight.' Kathleen paused, hoping for a moment that they could eat together, as they sometimes did after a long day. But Brel was busy tidying his desk, and ignored her remark. She put on her jacket. 'By the way, I checked on Miss Belmont. Her GP doesn't exist. There's no one of that name on the Register, let alone practising in the United Kingdom. The address and phone number she gave for him seem to belong to a department store in Penzance. And there's no trace of her own address or number. So what do we make of that?'

'God knows.'

'Perhaps your friend could help.'

'Perhaps. I'll certainly ask him.'

Brel put out the lights, locked the suite, said goodnight to Kathleen and took the lift to the top floor. Many years ago, when the house had been a private residence, the servants had slept in these attic rooms. Since then, by knocking down a couple of walls, they had been converted into a small but very attractive flat, which suited him admirably. No commuting to work. Within easy reach of Regent's Park and Primrose Hill when he wanted to walk off his frustrations. Convenient for the theatres, concerts, restaurants—all that London had to offer.

Admittedly, there were some strings attached. The rent was nominal, but whoever lived there was expected to take more than his fair share of nights and weekends on duty for the practice. Brel, without a wife or family, was admirably fitted for this. He preferred to be occupied, and had not found the work onerous. Most patients were reasonably considerate, and any inconvenience was more than offset by the flat itself.

As usual, he let himself into the hall with a feeling of

pleasure, heightened by the fact that he'd had a hard day. Barring emergencies, he didn't expect to be called out, and he was looking forward to a lazy evening, a couple of drinks, supper, music or television, and early to bed with a book. Fleetingly his conscience pricked him about Kathleen. He knew her husband was away on business and he could easily have invited her out to dinner. But he was glad he hadn't.

The phone rang. Resignedly Brel went to answer it. But it wasn't a patient, only Jack Dawson calling with an invitation for the following evening. Jack and his wife Marjorie were close mutual friends of his and Gerald's.

'Gerald's coming up to London a day early,' Jack said. 'He's dining with us. Why not come along, Brel?'

Brel hesitated. 'I'm on duty again,' he said finally, 'and Hampstead's a bit off my beat. I think I'd better stay here in case I'm called out. Thanks all the same.' Then he remembered, and added, 'Say, Jack, have you ever heard of a girl called Sally-Ann Belmont?'

'Never,' said Jack Dawson promptly. 'Why?'

'Oh, I met her today, and she claims to be a friend of Gerald's.'

'Well, she's news to me. But I don't know all his friends, girls or otherwise. You can ask him yourself tomorrow. He'll be staying at the club.'

'I might do that. Thanks.'

'See you on Thursday. Marjorie's hopping mad she can't come. She says pre-wedding stag parties went out with the ark.'

'I'm not sure I don't agree with her, but everyone seems very keen. Okay. Till Thursday, then.' Brel put down the receiver.

CHAPTER 2

The following afternoon Gerald Hinton was staring rather gloomily through his windscreen half way down the M4 between Reading and London. He would be in town for a couple of days before going to spend the weekend with his fiancée and his future in-laws.

Gerald was not as happy as a prospective bridegroom should have been. It was the coming weekend that worried him. He knew the Lydneys didn't approve of him, and in some ways he could see their point of view. There was no good reason why the rich, ambitious Archibald Lydney and his wife should consider him a suitable match for their only daughter. True, he'd inherited a considerable fortune from his father a year ago, together with a large printing firm in Reading and a most attractive house in a charming village nearby. But this seemed to count against him with Lydney, who was a self-made man. Then there was the age difference—he was fourteen years older than Elizabeth, but he kept himself in shape and was reasonably good-looking. He was kind and considerate and he loved Elizabeth and believed she loved him.

Oh, the hell of it, he thought. He'd forget about Elizabeth's parents till Saturday. There was plenty to enjoy before then, dinner with Marjorie and Jack Dawson this evening, his stag party tomorrow, perhaps a show on Friday if his hangover permitted it. He grinned to himself in anticipation.

Fond as he was of the Dawsons, Gerald chose not to stay with them on his visits to London. Hampstead wasn't sufficiently central for the things he wanted to do, and he preferred the Arts and Letters Club in the middle of Mayfair.

The Arts and Letters was a typical London men's club, though it had been one of the first to invite women to become members and share most of its premises. Not as well-known as the Garrick, its membership was very similar: writers, actors, publishers and people in related fields. Gerald had been put up for it many years ago by Peter Dale, a journalist friend, and Peter's brother, Terry, who directed television commercials. Gerald remained grateful to them. He found the club very useful, and well worth its ever-increasing subscription. Recently, he'd begun to take a hand in the club's administration, and had been elected to a couple of committees.

He put his car in a nearby garage, where space was reserved for members staying at the club, and carried his bag up the steps.

'Good afternoon, Mr Hinton, sir.' Roberts, the head porter, was on duty. He glanced at a list on his desk. 'Three nights this time, isn't it?'

'That's right.' Gerald smiled at him. 'I hope they've given me my usual room.'

'Yes, sir. Number 312. It's quite ready.' He handed Gerald a key. 'Just one bag, sir?' he asked.

'Yes. That's all right. I can manage it easily. Any messages?'

'No messages, sir. But a lady did telephone twice this morning. She seemed to know you were expected, but she didn't leave a name or number.'

'Thanks.' Probably Elizabeth, Gerald thought as he turned away, or Marjorie. He wondered vaguely what either of them might want.

On his way to the lift Gerald stopped to look at the new notices on the board. As he did so, he heard a voice at his elbow. 'Good afternoon, Mr Hinton.'

It was the club's new secretary, though 'new' was hardly the word any more: the man had been managing the club for the past six months. But, after the last secretary, who'd held the job for more than ten years . . .

' 'Afternoon,' Gerald said affably.

Gerald had first met Alan Jenson when, as a member of the club appointments committee, he had helped to interview him for the post. He had been an almost unanimous choice, an experienced catering and hotel manager, with a pleasant personality. Perhaps he spent less time in the bar with members than his predecessor, but that was no bad thing. Certainly the club was now run far more efficiently than in the past. Gerald turned his mind to more immediate matters. 'Everything set for my dinner tomorrow night?' he asked. 'All my guests are coming, as far as I know.'

'Oh yes. Everything's under control. We've put your party in the Irving Room. I hope you agree.'

'That'll be splendid! Thanks a lot.'

Gerald stepped into the lift and nodded goodbye to the secretary. The Irving Room would be ideal, he thought.

As soon as he reached his room, Gerald went to the phone beside the bed and asked the operator for Majorie's number.

'Gerald? Hello, dear. You're okay?'

'Yes, everything's fine. I just —'

'You are coming tonight? I mean, you're not calling to put us off?'

'No, Marjorie. Listen —'

Gerald explained, though it was already self-evident that it was not Marjorie who had been trying to contact him. Next he tried the Lydneys' number. A man's voice answered.

'Hello. This is Gerald Hinton. May I speak to Elizabeth, please?'

'Hi, Gerald! Nick here. How are you?'

'Fine, thanks. And you?'

'Absolutely whacked. Liz and I have been playing tennis all afternoon — singles — and we're both exhausted.'

'Aren't you working today?'

Gerald tried to keep the irritation from his voice, but failed and at once regretted it. Nick Ryle was Elizabeth's cousin, recently down from his university and now reading for the bar. As a schoolboy, when his parents were abroad, he had spent many of his holidays with the Lydney family, and had known Elizabeth all her life. What was more, Gerald suspected that Nick had at one time had an affaire with her. There was little doubt that he'd marry her, given the chance.

Nick said, 'It was such a lovely day I decided to play truant. After all, Liz is a lot more fun than the law.'

There was a pause. Such a remark wasn't calculated to set Gerald's mind at rest. He imagined Nick Ryle at the other end of the line in the big house near Tunbridge Wells, a large blond man in shorts and a tennis shirt, near to Elizabeth's age. More sharply than he had intended, Gerald said, 'Do fetch Elizabeth. I want to talk to her.'

'Okay.' Nick Ryle's voice could be heard shouting, 'Liz! Liz! Your revered fiancé wants to speak to you.' The voice returned to normal. 'She's in the kitchen getting us something cool to drink,' he explained. 'She won't be a minute.'

Gerald didn't answer. That was another thing that annoyed him about Nick. He always called Elizabeth 'Liz', as did her brother, though not her parents. Gerald himself had met her as Elizabeth, and always thought of her as that. Anyway, Liz didn't suit her. Beth, perhaps? But why shorten Elizabeth?

'Hello, Gerald.'

'Darling!'

By now Gerald no longer thought it was Elizabeth who

had phoned the club earlier. Nevertheless, he asked her and, when she denied it, said truthfully that in that case he couldn't imagine who'd been trying to reach him. He heard a murmur in the background and Elizabeth laughed.

'Nick says it must have been one of your other girl-friends.'

'Tell Nick if it was I'll pass her on to him now I've got you, darling.' Gerald tried hard to make his reply sound as light as Nick's comment, but he couldn't avoid feeling a slight tug of envy at Nick's long and close relationship with Elizabeth. Elizabeth herself, however, was chatting gaily about the forthcoming wedding, and they parted with mutual endearments.

Gerald hung up with vaguely mixed feeling. Damn Nick Ryle, he thought. It was absurd to be jealous of him, but he couldn't help it. He wished Ryle weren't coming to the party tomorrow, but obviously Elizabeth's brother had to be asked, and it had seemed impossible to invite Charles Lydney and not Cousin Nick.

Resolutely dismissing Ryle from his mind, Gerald unpacked, showered and shaved. It was still too early to go to Hampstead. He thought of having a drink at the bar and seeing who was around the club, but felt restless. Then he remembered John Breland, and again his hand went out to the phone. If Brel were free . . .

'My dear chap, I'm always pleased to see you,' Brel said, and meant it.

Brel liked Gerald Hinton. They had first met in Devon more than five years ago. Gerald had been on holiday with a friend and, climbing over rocks, had slipped and broken his ankle. By chance one of Brel's sisters saw the accident, and the whole Breland family had become involved. Excellent medical care, and what seemed to Gerald incredible personal kindness, had laid the foundation for a lasting friendship.

When Brel had subsequently moved to London, he'd been able to reciprocate. He invited Brel for weekends, introduced him to his friends, put him up for the Arts and Letters Club. Brel appreciated his help and attention.

'Here's to you — and to the wedding, Gerald.' Brel lifted his glass in salute. 'How are things going?'

Gerald paused, and drank before he answered. 'To be honest, I'll be glad when it's all over.'

Brel laughed. 'The groom always says that.'

'I know, but —'

Gerald stared out of the window at the rooftops opposite, and Brel sensed his friend's anxiety.

'What's the matter?' he said. 'Can you tell me?'

'Nothing really,' said Gerald. He hesitated, and added, 'I suppose it's a number of things.' Suddenly the welcome of the pleasant room, Brel's obvious concern, his own as yet unspoken doubts, all combined to overwhelm him for a moment. His feelings came out in a rush — the fact that Elizabeth's parents still seemed to regard him as an interloper, their son's patronizing attitude, the difference in age between himself and Elizabeth, the possessive familiarity with which Nick Ryle treated her . . .

'But what about Elizabeth?' Brel asked reasonably. 'After all, it's what she thinks that matters. She must want to marry you, or she woulnd't be defying her family. Though these days there's no way they could forbid the banns or anything. She's over age and she can do what she likes. Once the stress of the situation's over, and you're on your own away from her family, you should both be happy.'

'Sure, I know,' Gerald said. He smiled ruefully, mocking himself, and Brel grinned in return. He was glad that, having unburdened himself, Gerald seemed considerably more cheerful. Brel didn't profess to be any kind of psychiatrist, but he was sure that a conversation of this kind could do nothing but good.

Gerald was looking at his watch. 'I must be off. You know how Marjorie feels about her dinners. And I'm late already.'

The ringing of the phone bell interrupted them. Waving goodbye to Gerald, who muttered his thanks and let himself out of the flat, Brel listened intently to a husband anxious about his elderly wife whose gall bladder had been giving her trouble. It was some hours later, after the lady in question was safely tucked up in the London Clinic, that Brel thought again of Gerald, and remembered that he hadn't asked him if he'd ever met a Miss Sally-Ann Belmont.

Gerald enjoyed his evening. Marjorie had produced an excellent dinner, with a fine claret to accompany it. Pleasantly relaxed, he drove back to central London. He parked his car and rang the night bell of the club. As a security measure the doors were locked after midnight and the porter had to be summoned. There was a short delay before he arrived. It was Roberts, once again on duty.

'The lady telephoned again, sir,' he said at once. 'Twice, in fact. The second time she left her name.'

'Thanks,' Gerald said absently. He took the room key the porter was offering him, and the folded paper. Turning away, he said good-night over his shoulder.

'Good night, sir.'

Aware of the porter's curious gaze, Gerald crossed the hall and got into the lift. He waited till the doors closed, then unfolded the paper. He read, 'Miss Sally-Ann Belmont phoned at 1900 and 2200. No message.'

Sally-Ann Belmont? The name had been mentioned at dinner. He'd been talking of Brel when Jack had suddenly asked if he knew a Sally-Ann Belmont, apparently someone Brel had come across who claimed to be a friend. Naturally he'd said no.

Now it seemed that Miss Sally-Ann Belmont had phoned him four times during the day. Clearly she was determined to contact him. But why? he asked himself. And how could she know he was at the club? Or had she tried the office? And why hadn't she left a number?

In his room Gerald consulted the Directory beside the telephone. There were a few Belmonts, but no Sally-Ann, no S-A. So what? Doubtless the minor mystery would explain itself tomorrow. Gerald went to bed, but he was no longer so relaxed and it was some time before he slept.

CHAPTER 3

'I hope you approve, Mr Hinton.'

'Approve? Indeed I do. It looks splendid, absolutely splendid.'

They were standing by the wide double doors of the Irving Room, a large Victorian salon with brightly decorated plasterwork, overshadowed by the famous oil of Sir Henry in the role of Hamlet, gazing somewhat ominously along the length of the room from an end wall. Long windows, now covered with heavy cream velvet curtains, lined one side of the room, and on the opposite wall, between plaster pilasters, hung the club's well-known collection of early playbills.

Tonight a small bar had been arranged on a long table under Irving's painting, and two waiters were already standing by to serve Gerald's guests when they arrived. In the centre of the room was the table at which they would dine. Silver gleamed on the damask cloth. An array of glasses glistened by each place; Gerald had let himself be guided about the food, but he had chosen the wines himself. The menus were printed in gold. The candles were a golden yellow. The table napkins, folded to look like swans, each contained a yellow rosebud that could be slipped into a buttonhole. And in the centre, directly beneath the ornate chandelier, was an arrangement of yellow and white roses. The total impression was of gold and silver and white. Alan Jenson had excelled himself.

'Splendid!' repeated Gerald. 'It's very good of you to let me have the Irving Room when there are only fourteen of us.'

Alan Jenson smiled amiably. When he became secretary he had soon realized that pleasant and efficiently-organized private parties for members and their guests could be a useful source of revenue for the club, and he made it his business personally to supervise the arrangements for these functions. He did it well, with an unfailing flair for an occasion. And he had made a special effort for Mr Hinton.

'Not at all,' he said. 'The room was available for tonight, and it does have a certain air that some of the other rooms lack.'

Gerald Hinton felt a little embarrassed. Somehow a mere 'thank you' seemed a little inadequate for all the trouble the secretary had obviously taken. His predecessor hadn't been above accepting the gift of a few cigars or a box of golf balls for service beyond the call of duty, as it were, but this chap was different, and Gerald hardly liked —

Nevertheless, he looked at his watch and said. 'Let's have a drink together for once before my guests arrive.' He gestured towards the bar. 'What'll you have?'

For a second Alan Jenson hesitated. As a general rule he avoided drinking with members, but this was a special occasion. 'Thank you very much, Mr Hinton,' he said. 'I'd like that. A Scotch and soda, please.'

They moved down the room and a waiter poured a

whisky for Jenson and a gin and tonic — mostly tonic — for Gerald. He would have preferred no alcohol; he was going to have enough to drink that evening. But he couldn't seem churlish.

'Cheers!'

'To your future, Mr Hinton.'

'Thanks.' They each drank, then Gerald said, 'You're not married, of course.'

'No. I lived with my mother till she died eighteen months ago.'

Gerald nodded sympathetically and a little later the secretary finished his drink and said he had other duties to attend to. Left to himself, Gerald wandered over to the dinner table and looked around it, studying the place cards. Charles Lydney was on his right and Terry Dale on his left. Brel was facing him at the other end of the table.

Suddenly he decided that was not how he wanted it. Terry would get tight and tell increasingly risqué stories, and Charles would not be amused. Charles might be Elizabeth's brother, but he was a snooty bastard. He could sit where Brel had been placed, next to his pal, Nick Ryle, and as far from the head of the table as possible. Terry could swap with his brother, Peter, and . . .

Gerald had just completed his rearrangement when the guests began to arrive. The first were a couple of his old school friends who, it seemed, hadn't seen each other for years. After greeting Gerald and congratulating him, they at once began to exchange reminiscences. Then Jack Dawson came into the room with Brel.

Conversation became more general, and Brel said. 'By the way, Gerald, I meant to ask you last night. Have you ever met a Sally-Ann Belmont?'

'I asked him that, and he said no,' Jack remarked. 'None of us has ever heard of her. Who is this girl, Brel?'

'That's what I'd like to know,' Gerald said. 'Some

woman spent most of yesterdaying trying to phone me
here. It wasn't till I got back last night that I found she'd
finally left her name — Sally-Ann Belmont. Where did
you come across her, Brel — if it's the same girl?'

'It's not a very common name,' Brel pointed out. 'My
one came to me as a patient, recommended by her dear
friend Gerald Hinton. Have you called her back, Gerald?'

'No, I couldn't. She didn't leave a number — just a
name. And there's no likely Belmont in the book.'

'This is all a bit absurd,' Jack Dawson exclaimed.

'Absurd or not, it's what happened,' Brel said. 'You're
sure she's not an old girl-friend you've forgotten about,
Gerald?'

'Sure I'm sure. Bloody sure!' The words exploded from
Gerald with unexpected vehemence. 'Girl-friends I've
had, but not so many I'd completely forget one. I don't
take after my father.'

'Aha! The willing victim!'

A cheerful roar announced the arrival of Terry Dale.
With some relief Gerald broke off the conversation and
went to greet him and his brother. Jack Dawson turned to
Brel, still standing beside him. 'It's puzzling, this Belmont
business. What did she want with you?'

Brel hesitated. 'Oh, just a minor complaint,' he replied
tactfully.

At this point laughter grew in volume, as Terry Dale
continued to clown, treating Gerald as one about to
surrender all privilege on the altar of marriage. Others
had arrived, and Gerald found himself the centre of a
boisterous circle. It was a traditional stag party all right,
he thought.

On the fringe of the group Jack Dawson remarked in an
undertone to Brel, 'You know, that chap Terry always
astounds me. He jumps to it when his wife gives an order,
though you wouldn't think it from the way he behaves
when he's away from home. It's lucky his advertising job

gives him a good excuse to be out of town—or the country—so often.'

Brel was amused. 'I guess there are lots like that,' he said. 'Tell me, just what did Gerald mean about his father?'

'Father?'

'Yes. When he said he didn't take after him—about girl-friends, you remember. I've heard stories, of course, but I've never liked to ask Gerald the details.'

'There's no real secret about it. As you know, the old man died last year. He was over seventy, and his wife had died a couple of years before that. On the surface Gerald's father was a pillar of rectitude—read the lessons in church every Sunday and that sort of thing. It wasn't till Gerald was going through his papers that he found a bundle of hot-stuff love-letters. Apparently he'd had a succession of mistresses—one in particular he'd seen regularly for years. He'd even had an illegitimate son by her.'

'That must have been a shock for Gerald.'

'It was. He tried to trace the woman and her son—I don't know how seriously—but it was all a long time ago, and there was no clue to their surname, so he never got anywhere.'

'Too bad.' Brel found this family history interesting, but somehow inappropriate on such an occasion. He wished he'd not raised the subject, and looked round the room. 'Are we all here yet?'

'No, I don't think so.' Jack counted. 'Two missing. Lydney and Ryle.'

The invitation had said 7.15 for 8.00 p.m. Early, admittedly, but convenient for many, and certainly for the staff. A minute or two before eight o'clock Alan Jenson appeared at Gerald's elbow and asked if he were ready. Gerald hesitated. Neither Charles Lydney nor

Nick Ryle had yet arrived. On the other hand he couldn't delay dinner indefinitely.

'Okay. I seem to be minus two people, but we won't wait for them.' Controlling his irritation, he forced himself to smile at the secretary; it really was too bad of Lydney and Ryle. 'Go ahead,' he said. 'We're ready when you are.'

'Thank you.' Jenson crossed the room and spoke to the head waiter. The latter raised his voice. 'Gentlemen, if you would take your places. Dinner is served.'

The twelve of them sat down. Dinner began. Turtle soup was followed by bowls of *fruits de mer*. At this point, as the waiters withdrew, Charles Lydney and Nick Ryle arrived. Gerald did not stand up to welcome them.

Charles spoke first. 'Our apologies, Gerald. Our sincerest apologies. We really are sorry.'

'All my fault,' said Nick, and hiccuped.

Charles Lydney gave his cousin an exasperated glance. He was clearly embarrassed by their unpunctuality, whereas equally clearly Nick Ryle didn't give a damn.

'What happened?' asked Gerald politely, too politely perhaps. 'No trouble, I hope.'

Nick Ryle took it upon himself to answer. 'No. No trouble really. We stopped for a drink at a pub on the way and I was stupid enough to lock the car and leave the keys in the ignition. It's as simple as that.'

'It was bloody careless,' Charles said, not bothering to hide his annoyance. 'I'm truly sorry, Gerald.'

'Forget it, Charles.' Gerald waved a hand towards the empty chairs at the end of the table. He ignored Ryle. 'I'm afraid you've missed the soup, but I can recommend the sea-food.'

'Thanks.'

Nick Ryle said nothing. He followed his cousin to the table, sat and began to eat. The incident was over. Conversation resumed. Course succeeded course. Wine succeeded wine. Voices rose, laughter grew louder.

The table was cleared and coffee served. The waiters withdrew, and the port started circulating. At length Terry Dale pushed back his chair and, somewhat laboriously, rose to his feet.

'Unaccustomed—' he began, to be greeted with a roar of laughter. He stopped, grinned and started again. 'Well,' he said, 'perhaps I'm not as unaccustomed as all that. What I have to do, on behalf of you all, is propose a toast to our host, Gerald Hinton. I've known Gerald for many years, and till now he's managed to escape the trap of matrimony. Finally, he's been caught. Married men among us will commiserate. Gone will be his freedom, gone will be the happy days when he could please himself where he went, or when he came and went, when he could live without excuses, when he could . . .'

Terry Dale was in full flight. The rest of his speech was ribald, often obscene. It was greeted with gusts of laughter, interrupted by shouted comment, and applauded loudly when Terry finally collapsed into his seat.

'The toast,' Peter prompted him. 'You've forgotten the object of the exercise—the toast!'

Terry heaved himself up again. 'You're right.' He raised his glass. 'To Gerald! I give you Gerald—the latest to embrace the holy cow of matrimony.'

'To Gerald!'

It was a great shout, and it was followed by cries of, 'Speech! Speech!' With a broad smile splitting his face, Gerald rose.

'My friends,' he said. 'Thank you. Thank you very much indeed. I'm delighted you could all be here tonight to help me celebrate. And I mean celebrate. Because, in spite of Terry's dire warnings, I know I've got good reasons for celebration. In fact, I consider myself a very lucky man. As you know, I'm going to marry Elizabeth—'

'Oh no you're not!'

Gerald stopped in mid-sentence, his mouth agape, his body stiff with surprise, staring towards the double doors at the far end of the room. The men seated at the table swung in the direction of his gaze.

A girl stood in the open doorway, a waiter hovering ineffectually behind her. She came slowly into the room, and closed the door.

She said again, quite firmly, 'You're not going to marry her, Gerry. I intend to see that you don't.'

There was an audible gasp as the frozen tableau came to life. Brel looked round the table at his fellow guests. Jack Dawson had let his mouth drop open in amazement. Terry Dale, a glass of port clutched in an unsteady hand, looked stunned. Nick Ryle merely seemed amused. The others showed little reaction as yet, just a collective surprised blankness. Brel's impressions were no more than momentary, but they were to remain with him.

Gerald spoke first. 'What is this—some kind of joke? What—what are you talking about?' He paused, as if to swallow phlegm that was rising in his throat. 'Who are you?' he demanded.

'Darling, you know perfectly well who I am.'

Brel said, 'Miss Sally-Ann Belmont.'

She turned her bright blue eyes on him. 'That's right, Doctor. You know me, don't you, though we've only met once. You recognize me. And you'll confirm I'm pregnant, won't you?'

The whole table turned towards Brel, who could think of no appropriate response. He continued to stare at the girl, who really was beautiful, especially tonight, in a long gold dress of some metallic material that glinted as she moved. It was moulded closely to her body, but the gentle swell of her pregnancy was disguised by a flimsy stole, white with gold edging, that was draped around her shoulders. There was no doubt that Miss Belmont was striking. It suddenly occurred to Brel to compare her with Elizabeth Lydney; pretty as the younger girl was, there was no contest.

'What do you want?' Gerald was visibly losing his temper. His voice was becoming harsh with anger. 'What do you want?' he repeated. 'Who sent you here?'

'No one sent me, Gerry. I told you. I've come to warn you. I won't stand by and let you marry someone else, not while I'm carrying your child. So tell Liz, or whatever she calls herself, the wedding's off. If you don't, I'll — I'll turn up at the church and tell her myself.'

What had started as a tirade — Sally-Ann Belmont's eyes had been blazing — unexpectedly faltered. Brel had the distinct feeling that she had suddenly seen or heard or thought of something that had shaken her composure. Certainly she had been distracted.

'Rubbish! Nonsense! What the devil do you mean? What kind of game are you playing?' Gerald seemed beside himself with rage and frustration. He looked round at his friends. None of them was being of any help to him, not even Brel. 'What the hell are you after?'

'I've told you. It's quite simple. If you don't marry me, you won't marry anyone —'

'Now look here —'

It was a weak expostulation, but even so Gerald had wasted it. Miss Belmont had gone, sweeping out through the double doors as dramatically as she'd entered them. There was a moment's silence. Then Nick Ryle tittered.

It was enough. Gerald caught the suppressed snigger, and exploded. 'You — you utter shit! You laid that on! You —'

'I didn't,' said Ryle. 'It wasn't me. I swear it.'

Somehow, in spite of everything, Nick Ryle's reply carried conviction. 'Okay,' Gerald said. 'But I'm damn well going to find out who did. I'll bring that woman back and get the truth out of her.' As he spoke he was moving down the room. The doors slammed behind him and the murmur of comment turned into a babble. Everyone spoke at once.

'Not Gerald! It's some kind of hoax.'

'What a girl! Ravishing.'

'Poor old Gerald!'

'Poor old Gerald be damned. If he's been having it off with that bird he's to be envied.'

'Why the hell doesn't he marry her if she's so keen?'

'He happens to be marrying my sister — or he was — remember?'

'Then either your sister's an absolute rave, or she's putting the black on Gerald in some way. Look at the competition —'

'That's a bloody insulting remark!' Charles Lydney rose to his feet, knocking back his chair.

'Steady! Steady!'

'No need to take offence, old man. I'm sure your sister's a —'

'There's every need,' Nick Ryle intervened, half slurring his words. He stood up too, but carefully, pushing his chair back with a precise movement. He was at that stage of drunkenness when clarity and belligerence vie with each other. 'How dare you compare Liz to a tart! I'll teach you!' Picking up his glass of port, he flung its contents into the face of the man who had last spoken.

Dripping wine, the victim leapt to his feet, his fist raised. 'You stupid bastard!' he shouted.

'For heaven's sake, Nick, calm down. No one's saying anything about Elizabeth. Keep a grip on yourselves — both of you.' Jack Dawson tried to take charge. As Gerald's closest friend he felt it was up to him to deal with the situation, but it was hard to know what to do. It was only a few minutes since Sally-Ann Belmont had first appeared, but in that time the mood of the party had vastly changed. Dawson looked desperately at Brel for support.

Unexpected distraction came from Terry Dale, however. He staggered out of his chair and wove his way towards the door. Suddenly he stopped. 'Got to be — sick,' he said, and ran from the room, a hand clasped over his mouth.

Peter, his brother, hurried after him, followed by the man at whom Ryle had thrown the port, still mopping furiously at his shirt front with a table napkin. Charles Lydney had pulled Nick back into his chair, and they were muttering together. Someone said he had to pee. This eased the tension further, and there was a general exodus in the direction of the cloakroom.

John Breland found himself alone. He wandered over to one of the long windows, drew back the curtain and stared into the night. The young moon was covered by cloud, and the darkness was relieved only by street-lamps. Brel's first thought had been to follow Gerald, to help find Miss Belmont, to assist with questioning her, but something had restrained him — his professional involvement, perhaps. By now she had probably left the club, and Gerald could be anywhere. At least the porter should be able to throw some light on the circumstances of her arrival and departure.

Brel heaved a puzzled sigh. He knew it wasn't logical, but to some extent he blamed himself for what had happened. Maybe he should have been more forthcoming with Gerald about Miss Belmont, patient or not, instead of being so professionally bland. Perhaps he should have warned him. But about what? There was no way he could have known that the Belmont girl was going to be party to a gag of this kind.

A gag? A joke? Brel found it hard to believe that this was just a hoax. If so, it was a hellishly complicated one.

CHAPTER 4

As was only to be expected, Gerald Hinton's party never really recovered. Most of the guests reassembled — Peter Dale brought apologies from Terry, who was feeling ill — but it was a sense of obligation that brought them together, rather than any positive desire for each other's company. Standing around, they waited aimlessly for their host. No one had seen either Gerald or the girl since they had followed each other from the Irving Room.

'Terry all right?' Brel asked. 'Nothing I can do?'

'No — no, thanks. He feels rotten at the moment. He's just puked his heart out. Too much liquor and too much rich food. But he'll be fine. Luckily we arranged to spend the night at the club. It's a long drive to Richmond after a party, and neither of us can afford to be caught by the cops. Terry's only just got his licence back after being over the drink limit, and I've been done for speeding.' Peter grinned ruefully.

'Tough.'

'Anyway, we thought better safe than sorry, and a good thing too as it's turned out. Actually I wouldn't mind a bit of shut-eye myself. I know it's not late, but I've got a busy day tomorrow. Where the hell has Gerald got to?'

'Yes. Where is Gerald?' Charles Lydney joined them. 'If he doesn't come back soon, Nick and I are going to push off.'

'Ungrateful buggers,' Jack Dawson said to no one in particular. Charles turned towards him angrily, but Brel put a restraining hand on his arm. 'No, no,' Brel said soothingly. 'It's a difficult situation, but we're all in the same boat. Let's wait a while longer.'

Charles subsided, and Brel reflected that the situation

was more than difficult — it was quite absurd. Miss
Belmont had managed to ruin a good party, but
something might be saved if their host was to reappear. In
the meantime everyone had a sense of unease, of edginess,
of waiting for a bomb to explode. To himself, he echoed
Peter's words — where the hell was Gerald?

As if on cue, the double doors opened and Gerald
arrived. 'Sorry I've been so long. I've been dashing all over
the club.' He stopped, smiling weakly. 'What are you
doing? Not drinking, any of you? How about a nightcap?'
His cheerfulness was obviously forced.

There was a chorus of refusals. Gerald wiped the back
of his hand across his brow. He was sweating, Brel
noticed, and his eyes were very bright.

'Well, if you won't, I will.'

Charles Lydney said, 'But what about the girl, Gerald?
Did you find her?'

'No.'

The single syllable hung heavy for a moment. Then
Gerald turned on his heels and went over to the bar. The
others drifted after him. To keep him company and help
relieve the sudden tension, Brel asked for a whisky he
didn't want. Jack followed his lead. Someone else poured
himself a soft drink. But Charles Lydney insisted on
saying goodbye, and Nick Ryle went with him. Soon,
after Peter had again explained about Terry, the party
finally broke up, excuses of last trains and waiting wives
sounding vaguely insincere. No one liked to raise the
subject that was uppermost in all their minds. At last,
only Brel and Jack Dawson remained with Gerald.

'Gerald — this girl,' Jack Dawson said. 'Is she still in the
club? Did you ask the porter? Anyway, how did she get
into the place at all?'

'She asked for me,' said Gerald. 'The porter was a bit
surprised — he knew it was a stag party — but he was busy
and she seemed quite sure of herself, so he directed her to

the Irving Room. He didn't see her leave, but he's away from his post occasionally, and she could have slipped out. Probably she did. Anyway, I can't find her anywhere.' He sat down heavily and swallowed half his drink. 'Christ, it's a mess! I had to put a good face on it in front of the others, but I'm worried sick. What's Elizabeth going to think? Charles is sure to tell her — and the parents. If Charles doesn't, Nick sure as hell will. I haven't a hope. What can I say?'

'Tell them the truth,' Jack said a little impatiently. 'Say someone played you a wretched trick. It's the sort of thing that's done at stag parties. Say you'd never heard of the Belmont girl before yesterday, and never seen her till tonight.'

'I — I'm not sure that's the truth.'

'What on earth — '

'Somehow she looked familiar,' Gerald said miserably, 'though I can't imagine where I've seen her before.'

'Oh, for God's sake! Is that all? Of course you could have seen her before, or someone like her. It doesn't mean a thing. If you go on like this, you'll be admitting you fathered her brat next,' Jack said. He looked at his watch pointedly. He wanted to get away. The incident had been unpleasant at the time, but it was over now. At least, it would be over if Gerald didn't insist on making such an inordinate fuss about it. He turned to Brel. 'I suppose it's true? She is pregnant?'

Brel hesitated fractionally. Sally-Ann Belmont had been his patient, but she had lied to him and he certainly wouldn't treat her again. 'As she said, yes. She's pregnant all right — about sixteen weeks.'

'But not by me!' Gerald exclaimed. 'That's one thing I am positive about. And don't suggest I picked her up at a party and all I remember is a warm patch in the bed next morning, because it's just not so.'

Jack exchanged glances with Brel. 'Look here, Gerald,'

he said soothingly. 'You know perfectly well that this must be someone's idea of a pratical joke. Granted it's a pretty putrid joke, but there's no way it can be for real. I can't believe that Elizabeth — or any of the Lydneys — will take it all that seriously. Even the parents must have been young once.'

'That's not the point,' Gerald said bitterly. 'They'll seize on any excuse to turn Elizabeth off me — and back on to Nick Ryle, probably.' He drew a deep breath; it seemed to Brel that he was making a massive effort to control himself. 'I hope you're right, that it is just a joke, that it's not someone deliberately trying to stop me marrying Elizabeth. Because if it is, I swear —'

'Ryle? Could it be Ryle himself?' Brel hazarded, partly to distract Gerald from his rhetoric and partly because he wanted to see Gerald's reaction to the suggestion.

'Yes. Ryle. I've thought of that. With or without help from Charles. I know Nick denied it, but that doesn't mean a thing. He's the only one with any sort of motive.'

There was a moment's silence while Brel and Jack digested this comment. Then, abruptly, Jack Dawson said he must go. Brel lingered, partly because Gerald was so visibly upset, partly from curiosity. The more he thought about it, the less he was inclined to agree with Jack Dawson. He found it harder and harder to believe that Gerald was merely the victim of a hoax. The whole thing was much too elaborate. It all suggested considerable research and careful planning. There was something cold-blooded and purposeful, almost vicious, about the affair. It was certainly no juvenile prank.

'Come on, Gerald,' Brel said at last. 'You're not doing any good brooding over it. Maybe there'll be some explanation in the morning.'

They left the Irving Room together and walked along the corridor. At the top of the broad flight of stairs that led down to the hall they paused to say good-night. To one side of them was a bank of lifts, and beyond was the club library. On their other side a corridor led to a series of rooms, and off this, slightly secluded, was the main ladies' cloakroom. The sudden screams came from this direction.

They were shrill, high-pitched, hysterical, shattering the peace of the club. They ceased as abruptly as they had begun. A man's voice shouted for help.

Brel ran. Just outside the ladies' cloakroom he found an elderly man bending over the body of a woman. His face was very pale, paler even than the woman's. She had a bright red mark on her face.

'I slapped her,' the man said at once. 'I had to. She was screaming her head off.'

'I heard,' Brel said. 'Let me see. I'm a doctor.' He squatted down beside the woman, but she was already regaining consciousness, her eyelids fluttering. He put his fingers on her pulse for a few seconds, then sat back and smiled reassuringly up at the man. 'Your wife?'

'Yes.'

'Don't worry. She'll be all right. It was just a faint. She's coming round now.'

'Are you sure?'

'As far as I can tell. I'm sorry, my names Breland, John Breland.'

'Sencourt, Basil Sencourt,' said the elderly man absently. 'But why was she screaming? Margaret's never done anything like this before.'

'She'll tell us in a moment.' By now Gerald had arrived, and Roberts, the porter, with a waitress and a couple of club members. They were all standing around, looking helpless.

'Find me a cushion for her head,' said Brel, and one of the waitresses hastened to obey.

Brel rose to his feet, and as he did so his foot kicked

against a piece of porcelain that was lying on the carpet.
At once Roberts picked it up, his eyes going to a vacant
plinth in a corner of the wall by the entrance to the
cloakroom. It had once held a Chinese vase and, now that
attention had been drawn to the shadowed area, one
could see the other fragments of china partly hidden
behind the fluted wooden column.

Mr Sencourt knelt down with the cushion, as Roberts
said, 'Did Mrs Sencourt knock it over when she fell?'

'No, she didn't,' Sencourt said firmly. 'It was broken
already. I noticed it while I was walking up and down
here, waiting for Margaret to change. I thought the vase
had been broken earlier, and the bits brushed into the
corner till tomorrow.'

'Basil!' Mrs Sencourt was struggling to sit up, and Brel
gently pushed her back, taking her wrist in his fingers
again. 'A glass of water, perhaps,' he said to the porter.

'Yes, sir.'

Immediately the waitress moved towards the ladies'
cloakroom, only to stop in surprise as Mrs Sencourt cried,
'No! Don't!'

By now Mrs Sencourt had pushed off Brel's restraining
arm, and was sitting on the floor. She looked a sensible
woman, hardly given to hysteria. In a low, clear voice she
said. 'Don't go in there for a minute. I'm sorry to have
been so stupid, but I was shocked. There's a body in the
ladies' cloakroom, in the bath in the further dressing-
room.'

For a moment there was a stunned silence. No one
moved. Then Brel strode into the cloakroom. He paused
inside the doorway. To his left was an area with lavatory
cubicles, washbasins and dressing-tables. Immediately
ahead of him was a counter behind which the attendant
usually sat, though no one was on duty now. On the wall
immediately to his right were rows of coat-hangers, and
opposite them, beside the attendant's counter, were

several doors, one of which was open. The décor was a rather overwhelming deep pink—high gloss paint or tiles—and the general impression was of a search for prettiness and femininity.

'In there, sir?' Roberts, who had followed closely on Brel's heels, pointed to the open door. 'Those are the dressing-rooms for ladies. Ladies can have a bath and change there if they're up from the country for the day. They can leave their things there too. Mrs Sencourt was using one.'

Brel nodded. He pushed at the half-open door and it swung back on its hinges, revealing the interior of the small room. Again everything was pink, dressing-table, washbasin, bath, shower curtain. On a stool was an overnight bag, a silver evening sandal poking from it. There were a few cosmetics on the dressing-table. A green evening dress lay in a heap on the floor, beside the other sandal. As Mrs Sencourt was to explain to the police later, she had changed into her day clothes and was packing to go home, when the drip of the bath tap had made her draw back the shower curtain and she had seen . . .

Brel saw exactly what had shocked Margaret Sencourt—the woman lying in an empty bath. Mrs Sencourt had recognized her at once as the cloakroom attendant who had been on duty that evening, but to Brel she was a stranger. Only the neat black skirt and the once-white blouse suggested to him that she was a member of the club's staff. Her face was contorted and her neck was almost certainly broken. And, to judge from the bright blood on the front of the blouse, she had also been stabbed or shot.

Behind him Brel heard the porter gag. 'Christ! It's Dora Brown. Who—who'd ever do that to Dora?'

There was a rising murmur of voices, as Gerald and the others crowded into the cloakroom. Brel turned sharply to Roberts, acting almost instinctively. 'Keep everyone

out of here,' he said at once. Call an ambulance and the
police. Get Mr Jenson. Put someone on the front door to
see that no one leaves the building.'

Glad of the clear orders, the porter hastened to obey.
As the onlookers were ushered firmly back into the main
corridor, Brel knelt beside the bath. He was morally
certain his call for an ambulance was pointless, for Dora
Brown was dead, but he had to go through the motions.
No pulse. No respiration. The neck at an impossible
angle to the trunk. A wound over the heart, no longer
bleeding.

Brel knelt back and regarded the body. It was almost
the first time since his student days in a hospital casualty
department that he had been confronted with unnatural
death. The woman had been in her fifties, he guessed, a
small, frail creature. She looked as if, in life, she might
have had some of the perkiness of a sparrow. Now she was
dead, clearly dead. Whoever had killed her had made
quite sure of it.

Had she been knifed or shot? Quite apart from the
unlikelihood that the sound of a shot would have passed
unnoticed in the club, the clean edges of the slit at the
centre of the bloody patch on the blouse strongly
suggested the former. In addition, to judge from the
terrified expression on her face, Dora Brown had known
she was about to die. Perhaps she had been knifed first
and then thrown into the bath, breaking her neck
inadvertently.

Now, time of death? Carefully Brel laid his hand on her
cheek in an effort to estimate her temperature. Warm,
but the room was warm. Then, slowly, he began to draw
aside her blouse in order to examine the wound more
closely.

'Don't touch her!'

Startled, Brel jumped to his feet. He had been so
engrossed in his investigations that he hadn't heard

footsteps or sensed anyone coming into the room. He felt embarrassed, as if he had been caught acting suspiciously in some way.

Alan Jenson said, 'I'm sorry, Dr Breland. I didn't mean to speak sharply. But I gather it's not an accident. If you're sure she's beyond help, I don't think the police will want her touched more than necessary.'

'No, you're quite right.' Brel had regained his composure. 'In any case it's none of my business. I was just curious.'

'Yes, of course, being a doctor. It's very lucky you were here.'

Brel watched the secretary's eyes darting about the bathroom, and saw his involuntary shiver as finally and reluctantly his gaze came to rest on the dead woman. Dora Brown was not a pretty sight. And she had been one of Jenson's staff, so he would have known her relatively well. He had a right to be shaken.

When Jenson spoke again, however, his voice was reasonably steady. 'If there's nothing more you can do, I suggest we leave her, Doctor. The police should be here soon.'

'They've been called? Good!'

'Yes. I was in bed when Roberts came to my room, and he phoned while I threw on some clothes. The porter's waiting for them in the hall now. We're only a few minutes from West End Central station in Savile Row, so the officers shouldn't be long. He'll bring them up as soon as they arrive.'

Brel nodded. He had already noticed the pyjamas over which the secretary had hastily pulled a pair of trousers and a jacket. He said, 'I'm afraid this is a shock for you, and bad news for the club.'

Jenson nodded silently, and led the way out of the dressing-room. Brel watched with some surprise as the secretary went to the far end of the cloakroom, produced a bunch of keys, and locked what had appeared to be the door of another dressing-room.

'What's through there?' Brel asked.

'It's a service door, and I want to be certain that no one comes in here that way. It's really meant for staff use, but sometimes ladies use the service area as a short cut from the drawing-room.'

As he spoke, Alan Jenson, showing considerable foresight, was collecting the few coats and wraps that remained on the hangers, and folding them over his arm. Then with a glance round as if to assure himself that everything was in order, he ushered Brel from the cloakroom to face the group of people gathered in the corridor outside.

CHAPTER 5

The group had increased in number. Two ladies had arrived in search of their coats. Their husbands hovered in the background. The night porter had just come on duty and was wanting to know what had happened. Someone had brought Mrs Sencourt a chair, and she was the centre of attention.

In the past, Brel's reaction to the secretary had been one of indifference, but during the next few minutes he found much to admire in Alan Jenson. Jenson had clearly, and reasonably, been appalled by the sight of Dora Brown's body, but he showed no sign of emotion as he emerged from the cloakroom to confront the collection of club members and staff. He was, or he seemed to be, calm and self-contained, and he was certainly as efficient as ever.

'Ladies and gentlemen,' he said quietly but crisply, and conversation ceased. 'I'm sorry to have to tell those of you who don't already know, but there's been a tragic occurrence. A member of the staff has died in one of the dressing-rooms. The circumstances are such that I've had no alternative but to call the police. They should be here shortly. In the meantime I must ask that none of you leaves the club.' He turned to the night porter. 'Roberts is still in the front hall, isn't he?'

'Yes, sir.'

'But that's absurd — keeping us here, I mean.' A big florid-faced man protested. 'We know nothing about this — this occurrence as you call it. My wife merely wants to get her wrap.'

'I'm sorry, Sir Richard. Naturally I can't prevent you from leaving, but it would be a great help if you didn't insist. Apart from the members spending the night here, there must be very few members left in the club by this time. If you leave, they'll all want to leave too, and the police will think we're not cooperating — which won't do the club any good.'

'I see. Very well.' Sir Richard Wander was Chairman of the Arts and Letters Management Committe, and Jenson's had been a subtle appeal. 'What do you want us to do?'

'I suggest you assemble in the small drawing-room — the Milton Room. I'll arrange for drinks to be served, or tea or coffee — anything you wish. And if anyone would prefer to stay overnight — if they're likely to miss a train, for instance — I'll see that accommodation's available.' He managed a wry smile. 'Fortunately we're not full at the moment.'

'Splendid!' Sir Richard said. He seemed to have forgotten his earlier objections. 'Come along, everyone. We'll leave it all in our secretary's capable hands.'

With an imperious gesture Sir Richard led away his followers, Mrs Sencourt on her husband's arm. Gerald went with them, looking either dazed or lost in thought, and Brel was about to join him when he felt Alan Jenson's hand on his shoulder.

'Please, Dr Breland. I need your help. There aren't many staff on the premises at this time of night. I've got to organize refreshments and rooms — I'm sure the Sencourts will want one; she must have had a dreadful shock. Roberts is on the front door, as you know, and I want the night man to do his usual rounds, make sure everything is all right. Would you stay here till the police come, and stop anyone who tries to go into the cloakroom?'

Brel had no choice but to acquiesce. He straddled the chair that had been brought for Mrs Sencourt, and waited. He realized the uselessness of speculation, but inevitably his thoughts turned to Dora Brown and her violent — almost ferocious — death. Someone must have hated her a lot, or been extraordinarily angry.

Restless, Brel abandoned his chair. This short cul-de-sac that led only to the ladies' cloakroom was not a part of the club known to him. He could never remember seeing the vase that had been broken. Idly, he picked up one of the larger pieces, and examined it carefully. He was no expert, but he thought it was Chinese and reasonably valuable, though not a great treasure or it probably wouldn't have been hidden away in a corner.

The large glass display cabinet against the opposite wall was more interesting. Black doublet, hose and cape, a sword and dagger. According to the notice the costume had been worn and the properties used by Gielgud in one of his performances as Hamlet. Given the present passion for collecting such theatrical memorabilia, this lot should fetch a tidy sum at auction.

Brel's mind was only casually involved with the display, and it was by mere chance that he noticed the cabinet was unlocked. One of the large glass doors was very slightly open. With the nail of his first finger, Brel began to pry at it.

'Dr Breland!'

Brel swung round. He was conscious that for the second time that night the secretary had rather embarrassingly caught him with his curiosity showing, but he didn't apologize. Instead, he looked beyond Jenson to the men behind him.

'The police? Good,' he said, hoping that Jenson would ignore the open cabinet.

The secretary, however, was not to be distracted. 'Was that door unlocked again, Doctor.'

'It was unlocked, yes.'

'Is this important?' The man who spoke was obviously the more senior of the two officers. 'I'm Detective-Inspector Crewe.' He introduced himself. 'And Detective-Constable Green.' He looked enquiringly at Brel.

'Dr John Breland,' the secretary said. He had moved quickly to the cabinet and was staring at its contents. 'No. It's not important, Inspector. There's nothing missing. It's just that the cabinet door should be kept locked, but the staff are careless, and when they clean—'

'Quite.' The Inspector cut Alan Jenson short. 'Now, may I see the body?'

'Of course. Through there. To your right. In the second dressing-room.' Jenson didn't offer to accompany him.

The Inspector paused and turned to Brel. 'You've already examined her, I gather, Dr Breland. The police surgeon will be here soon and he'll certainly want to have a word with you. And you can tell us how much you moved the body.'

'I scarcely touched it,' said Brel. 'There was really no doubt, no need . . .'

'Fair enough,' interrupted the Inspector. 'But show me, anyhow.'

As they moved into the cloakroom, Brel suppressed a grin. The secretary clearly resented the somewhat curt and acerbic attitude of the detective-inspector. After all, Jenson was more than a mere employee of the club; he was its chief executive.

'Inspector, as the club secretary . . .' he began.

'Thank you.' The Inspector kept his voice neutral, but his chin came up formidably. 'For the moment, just wait here, please.'

The Inspector stood in the door of the dressing-room and took in the scene in a couple of minutes. However aggressive he might appear, he was no fool. He asked two questions.

'That's how she was when you first saw her, Doctor?'

'Yes,' said Brel. 'As you can see, death was obvious, but I went through the routine and felt for the vital signs. It was no use. I didn't even examine the wound.'

'Fine,' said the Inspector. 'And time? Did you think about how long she might have been dead?'

'Er—yes, I did,' said Brel. 'But it's not really my line. The flesh was warm when I touched her, but so was the room, of course. I think you'll need the police surgeon and the pathologist for that.'

'Yes,' said the Inspector. 'Well, at least one thing's obvious. She didn't slip in the bath and do that damage to herself, did she? We'll get the Yard at once.' He issued a series of rapid instructions to the detective-constable, who promptly disappeared, presumably in the direction of their radio car. To Brel, the Inspector said, 'They'll all be here in a few minutes. In the meantime, we'll get the place organized.'

Detective-Inspector Crewe was as good as his word. In a very few minutes Brel found himself in the Milton Room with Gerald, Mr and Mrs Sencourt and the other more or less reluctant witnesses who had been up and about in the club when the police arrived; they were all under the slightly embarrassed eye of a uniformed constable seated by the door. No one knew whether the Scotland Yard officers had arrived yet, but it was understood that the secretary was rousing the few members who had slept blamelessly in their beds throughout the confusion, and warning them to get dressed and be prepared to answer questions.

In the Milton Room there was little conversation. It turned out that Mrs Sencourt—the crucial witness who had found the body under such distressing circumstances—had already been briefly interrogated. Apart from Brel, who remained largely silent, the others had little to offer, though one woman said she had popped into the cloakroom about nine-thirty, and the attendant had been alive and well then.

'She was okay later than that,' Gerald muttered to Brel.

'What? How on earth do you know?'

Gerald cast a warning glance towards the policeman by the door. Brel looked at his friend anxiously. As the host, Gerald had drunk a lot in the course of the evening, and he was still drinking now, a half-empty glass in his hand.

'You're going to have a hell of a hangover in the morning, Gerald,' Brel said quietly.

'Sufficient unto the day. And tomorrow can't be worse. Christ! What an end to my party!' He waved a hand vaguely at the rest of the room. 'For that matter, what a party!'

'But Dora Brown, Gerald—when did you see her?'

'Who?'

'Dora Brown, the woman who's been killed.'

'Oh, her. Well, when I went after that bitch, Sally-Ann Whatnot, I thought I saw her disappear into the ladies' and I waited for her to come out. That's partly why I was away so long. She didn't appear, but I could see this Dora Brown sitting behind her counter. I beckoned her out and asked if a girl in a gold dress was in there. She said no, I must have been mistaken. So I gave up and took myself off.'

Brel thought of the service door next to the dressing-rooms and wondered if Miss Belmont knew of the other way out and had told the attendant to keep quiet about her exit. Any simple story—a man she wanted to avoid—would have done the trick. He said, 'Are you sure it was Dora Brown you spoke to?'

Gerald shrugged. 'A little woman, scrawny, in her fifties.'

'That sounds right. You'll have to tell the police, Gerald. Can you fix the exact time?'

'Probably. It can't have been more than a few minutes after I followed that wretched girl out of the Irving Room—it would have been just before ten, say.'

'That could be important, you know.'

'Yes. But I can't tell the police all about Sally-Ann Belmont or whatever her name was. It would just confuse the situation and make me look stupid. I suppose I could say I was searching for a friend, or something. And where the hell are the police, anyway? How much longer are they going to keep us cooped up here?' Gerald was suddenly irritable. 'I want to go to bed,' he added wearily.

The door opened and there was a sudden squeak as the constable pushed back his chair and stood up. Inspector Crewe came into the room, raising his hand for silence. Not a very likeable character, Brel thought again, but undoubtedly efficient.

'Detective Chief Superintendent Freeman and his team have arrived from New Scotland Yard,' the Inspector said. 'He apologizes for not greeting you at once, but he's gone straight to the scene of the death. Mr Jenson has helped me prepare a list of members and guests and staff who were on the club premises this evening, and the Chief

Superintendent would like to see those of you who are still here individually, starting with Mrs Sencourt. He emphasizes these will only be brief preliminary interviews, to enable him to grasp the affair generally. Formal statements can wait till tomorrow morning.'

There was a chorus of objections. Basil Sencourt insisted on being present while his wife was interrogated. Sir Richard Wander demanded priority; he had waited quite long enough. Others pointed out loudly that they knew nothing about Dora Brown or her death or murder or whatever it was. Calmly the Inspector dealt with the protests, reiterating that the immediate interviews were vital to the investigation, but would not take long. Brel said nothing. He knew he had no valid excuse; he had been the doctor on the spot at the wrong moment. His patience was rewarded. Turning to him, Inspector Crewe added, 'Would you come with me too, Dr Breland? Dr Forsyth, our police surgeon, would like to consult with you before you see the Superintendent.'

In the event it was Forsyth who ushered Brel into the small smoking-room where Chief Superintendent Freeman had established himself. In spite of the alleged informality of the occasion Brel noticed a second plain-clothes officer sitting at a side table with a notebook open in front of him.

The Chief Superintendent stood up as the two doctors came in. He offered his hand to Brel, a huge hand. Even John Breland, himself by no means small, felt dwarfed beside the towering figure of Detective Chief Superintendent Mike Freeman. Well over six feet in his socks and proportionately broad, he looked like a rugger full-back; indeed, in his younger days he had been twice capped for England. Now, in his mid-forties, he had put on weight, but he was still impressive.

'Dr Breland, I'm pleased to meet you. I'm even more

pleased you happened to be on the spot. And I know Forsyth is.'

Forsyth was older and greying. 'Indeed,' he said. 'There's nothing like an immediately available expert witness to give a second opinion.'

Brel looked at the officer with the notebook. 'Ah,' said Freeman. 'That's Detective-Sergeant Anderson — Bill Anderson. I'd never get anywhere without him. Don't worry about the few notes he's taking. We'll have to get everything down properly tomorrow.'

Brel grinned. He liked them both — and the doctor. He could see at once that the apparent informality was a useful ploy; many witnesses would be more forthcoming immediately after the event and in circumstances like these.

'Well,' said Freeman. 'What can you tell us? You were here at a party, I gather. Though you are a member of the club?'

'Yes,' said Brel. 'I have been for some years. The party was for an old friend who's getting married shortly. It was while he was seeing me out that we heard Mrs Sencourt scream.' Brel explained briefly the sequence of events, but he made no mention of Sally-Ann Belmont, nor of Gerald's conversation with Dora Brown. He confined himself strictly to his own actions and observations.

'As far as the body's concerned, I think Dr Forsyth agrees that she was knifed or stabbed and then thrown violently into the bath. The broken neck was incidental, even accidental. It wouldn't have taken great strength; she was only a little thing,' he added.

Forsyth nodded. 'That's right. I've nothing to add. And there's no help from body temperature about time of death. You'll have to see what you get from witnesses and the PM.'

'What about the weapon?' Brel looked at the Chief Superintendent.

'We certainly haven't found it,' Freeman said. 'It wasn't in the bathroom or the cloakroom or anywhere obvious. I guess you know as well as we do what it must have been like — a knife or a dagger with a blade about —' He stopped and cocked an eyebrow at Brel. 'What is it, Doctor? Have I said something?'

Brel, who could have sworn that his expression hadn't changed, was surprised at the acuteness of the Chief Superintendent's observation. He said slowly. 'Well — yes. It was just a mad idea.'

'Tell me. At this stage of the game all ideas are welcome, mad or otherwise.'

'You mentioned a dagger. In the corridor outside the cloakroom there's a glass cabinet containing a costume that Gielgud wore as Hamlet — and the sword and dagger he used.'

'A real dagger? I thought they had rubber ones or collapsible ones on the stage.'

'Not this time. I'd swear it's real. The director must have been a stickler for realism. What's more, it seems that one of the cleaners left the cabinet unlocked — but you must ask the secretary about that.'

'I certainly will. Thanks a lot.' Freeman smiled grimly. 'It's just possible you're on to something. Bill,' he said to the sergeant, 'just go up and make sure the chap on duty outside the cloakroom keeps a special eye on that cabinet.'

'It's still there — the dagger,' Brel said. 'Or it was when Inspector Crewe and the first lot of police arrived. But as far as I could see it looked perfectly clean. There was certainly no obvious blood on it or around it.'

'The dripping tap!' Dr Forsyth said unexpectedly.

'What?' Brel didn't understand.

'What he means, Doctor,' Freeman said, 'is that our villain could have cleaned the dagger in the bath. Which would account for the fact that the tap was left dripping on the late Mrs Brown.' Again the Chief Superintendent smiled his attractive broad smile. 'Or of course he might just have been washing his hands.'

'You think she might have been killed outside the cloakroom and carried in?' Brel said thoughtfully. 'There wouldn't have been much blood till the weapon was pulled from the wound. And that might account for the broken vase. You do know about the vase, Chief Superintendent?' he asked.

'We do. Mr Sencourt told us the story. It could be relevant, and it might help with the time of the murder. But it's all very "iffy" at this stage. We know so little. It's really a question of collecting—' He broke off. 'What the hell's that?'

Their conversation was interrupted by a loud bumping outside the door. Then suddenly it flew open. A uniformed constable came in, dragging a struggling man. The man, apparently in his mid-twenties, was small but tough. Though he was handcuffed he was giving the policeman a bad time. Behind them hovered Alan Jenson.

'Stand still!' It was like the roar of a bull.

The man ceased struggling as if pole-axed. He stayed quite still and stared, open-mouthed, at Chief Superintendent Freeman who rose slowly to his full height, thrust his head forward and stared back. It was no contest.

'Now,' the Chief Superintendent said, 'who the hell are you? And what are you doing in this club, obstructing the police in the execution of their duty?'

The small man was frightened, but not completely intimidated. 'I'm Doug Brown,' he said. 'I've come to see my ma. I've a perfect right to—'

'You've no right whatsoever,' Alan Jenson interrupted. 'These are private premises. I've told you before. I won't have you—'

'Please!' It was a command, not a request. The secretary was silent and the Chief Superintendent turned to the uniformed man. 'Where did you find Mr Brown?'

'He was climbing out of a back window of the club, sir.'

'Ah! That's rather unusual behaviour. And why were you doing that, Mr Brown?'

'I told you, I came to see my ma. I used to work here till he sacked me,' Doug Brown raised his cuffed wrists at Jenson and glared at him. 'Said I was lazy. Proper little sergeant-major he is. Anyway, I know my way round the club.' With a sudden access of courage he added, 'And I'm not saying any more till you take these things off of me.'

The Chief Superintendent nodded and the handcuffs were removed, though the constable stayed close beside Brown.

'And did you see your ma?' asked Freeman. 'I take it you mean Mrs Dora Brown?'

'Dora Brown? That's right, yes. No. I didn't see her. I stood outside the door of the ladies' and gave a whistle, like. It was awkward, being the ladies'. I couldn't very well go in. Usually my ma comes out when she hears me, but tonight she didn't. So I went away and waited a bit in the pantry downstairs, and then all you cops started to arrive. I couldn't get out of the front, and the staff doors were all locked. So I thought I'd nip out of a window. That's when he caught me.'

It was a long speech. To Brel it didn't ring altogether true. On the other hand, it was difficult to believe that Brown was aware his mother was dead. The Chief Superintendent seemed to reach the same conclusion.

He said, 'Constable, fetch Mr Brown a chair. I'm sure he's sorry for the trouble he's caused, and we'll say no more about it for the moment. Then you can see Dr Breland out. We'll have a draft statement typed up,

Doctor. You can come in and look at it and sign it tomorrow.'

'I have patients all day, Chief Superintendent. Would early evening do?'

'Well, yes. But as soon as possible. Give my office a call in the morning and we'll fix a time. Good night, and many thanks.'

Forsyth echoed the good night, but Brel went almost reluctantly. He would have liked to know more about Doug Brown, and in particular he would have liked to assure himself that Gerald was all right. But the constable saw him to the door of the club, and he had no option but to depart.

CHAPTER 6

The telephone rang, and rang again. Gerald Hinton dredged himself up from the depths of sleep. Reluctantly he stretched an arm from under the blankets, picked up the receiver and propped himself on one elbow. Instantly a sharp pain stabbed through his head, so acute that for a moment he thought he would be physically sick on the floor. Brel had been right, he thought; this was the most almighty hangover.

'Hello! Hello! Are you there, sir?'

Gerald swallowed hard and suppressed the angry crack that rose to his lips. Where the hell did they expect him to be? 'Yes. What is it?' he said finally.

'It's the porter here, sir. There's a Mr Lydney and a Mr Ryle to see you. They're in the hall.'

'They're what? At this time of the morning!'

'It's past ten, sir.' Gerald glanced at his watch. The porter was right. It was a few minutes after the hour. Then he groaned aloud as the full horror of yesterday

evening came flooding back. The dead woman in the
bath. Poor wretch! The Belmont girl; obviously that was
what Lydney and Ryle wanted to see him about.
Involuntarily his groan turned into a whimpering noise
deep in his throat.

'I'm sorry, sir. What did you say?'

Gerald made an effort to pull his thoughts together.
'I'll be down in twenty minutes. Give them some coffee in
the Coffee Room while they're waiting, will you?'

'Yes, very good, sir. I think the police have finished in
there.'

The police. Oh God! He'd forgotten them. Today he'd
have to make a formal statement, and he'd need his wits
about him. He shivered convulsively, but with an effort
slid out of bed. He nicked himself twice shaving, and
swore volubly. He felt ghastly; sharp pains were still
shooting through the top of his head. But he managed to
get dressed, take some aspirin and make his way
downstairs.

He found Lydney and Ryle in the Coffee Room — a
large, comfortable salon on the ground floor of the club,
where coffee was available eighteen hours a day. He
poured himself a cup, black, and carried it across to the
two men.

' 'Morning, Nick, Charles.' Gerald made no attempt to
smile as he sat down beside them. 'This is an unexpected
visit. What —'

Without preamble Charles Lydney interrupted.
'Gerald, we want the truth about Sally-Ann Belmont. As
Elizabeth's brother I think I've got a right to know —'

'Do you? And what right has Nick got?' Gerald turned
angrily on Nick Ryle. 'It was you that laid on this thing
with the girl, wasn't it? You denied it last night, and I was
inclined to believe you. But you were lying. It's the only
reasonable explanation. You want to marry Elizabeth
yourself, and you're prepared to play any grubby trick to

get your hands on her.'

'That's bloody well not true!' Ryle's voice had risen, and another club member, buried behind his paper, coughed reprovingly. Ryle dropped his voice. 'It's not true,' he repeated, biting off each word for emphasis. 'Sure, I want to marry Elizabeth. I always have. Everyone knows that. I thought it was understood between us. Maybe I took her too much for granted—' He broke off, then shook his head. For a moment Gerald almost liked him.

'But if you had nothing to do with it,' he said more mildly, 'why did you find it so funny? You were roaring your stupid head off. I saw you.'

'Because it was funny. Because I thought someone—not me, but someone—was playing a hell of a good joke on you. Damn it, Gerald, there she was—this Belmont girl in her gold dress, just like that TV ad, and matching all the decorations. Of course I thought it was some kind of spoof. It wasn't until she started talking about the child that I began to wonder. That was going a bit far.' Slowly Nick Ryle added, 'I'm still wondering.'

'And so am I,' said Charles Lydney. 'If this girl's going to have your brat, Liz'll take a pretty dim view. And so will I. And our parents. Okay, your past is your past, but this is your bloody present.' Charles stopped suddenly. 'Gerald, are you listening?'

'Yes, I heard,' Gerald said. 'I heard Nick too. What he said about the television advertisement. I remember it clearly. It was for chocolates. Each bit was wrapped in gold paper, and the tag line was, "Give your golden girl a box of Gold." It created quite a stir three or four years ago. And I believe Nick's right. Sally-Ann Belmont was the golden girl. Maybe Terry Dale would know . . .'

Charles Lydney exchanged exasperated glances with his cousin. 'Gerald, listen,—'

'No, you listen to me for once, Charles.' Gerald seemed to have woken from a trance. He finished his coffee and

stood up purposefully. His head still ached, but somehow
the pain had receded into the background of his
emotions. 'Look, I'm going to take your word and Nick's
that neither of you was responsible for this business of
Sally-Ann Belmont. Okay. In return you've got to take
mine that what she said was a tissue of lies. I'm coming to
stay with you and your family tomorrow, and I'll tell
Elizabeth myself what happened at the party. You can
have your say then, in front of me — but not before. Is
that fair? Is that agreed?'

Charles Lydney shrugged. 'Very well, though I don't
see what difference it's going to make.'

'It may make all the difference in the world. By then I
may have located Miss Sally-Ann Belmont and wrung the
truth out of her.'

'In twenty-four hours? You've got a hope! Unless you
know where to start looking for her,' Nick Ryle said
unpleasantly.

'At least I've got an inkling,' said Gerald. 'And I owe
that to you, Nick.'

'Do you? Well, good luck,' said Ryle sarcastically.

'Thanks all the same.' Gerald looked at his watch. 'I'm
sorry, but you'll have to excuse me. I've got a lot to do,
including making a statement to the police about the
murder we had here last night.'

'What? Don't tell me you've managed to get yourself
involved in that business the porter was talking about.
What on earth's it got to do with you?'

'No more than with anyone else who was here. For that
matter, I imagine the police'll want to see you two, when
they get around to it. They've got a complete list of
everyone who was in the club for any reason yesterday
evening.'

'Still —' Charles Lydney sounded exasperated — 'you
really are the most — the most —'

'Unsatisfactory brother-in-law you can think of,

Charles? Too bad,' Gerald snapped. 'You wouldn't be my
choice, either. So I'll see you tomorrow. Now, as you're
guests in my club, I'll show you out.'

As soon as he had got rid of Lydney and Ryle, Gerald
Hinton went to speak to the porter on duty. 'Good
morning, Roberts,' he said. 'You still here?'

'I got away about one this morning, sir, but I thought
I'd better come in early today, with the police all over the
club.'

'Not quite everywhere, surely.'

Gerald's was a meaningless remark, but the porter
grunted and looked sourly at a very young, uniformed
constable who had just walked across the hall as casually
as if he were a founder-member of the Arts and Letters.
'Bloody fuzz,' Roberts muttered under his breath.

'Are they getting anywhere, do you think, the fuzz? The
police, I mean,' Gerald asked.

Hurriedly recollecting himself the porter said, 'About
poor Dora. Yes, sir, I think so. From what I've heard,
they seem to suspect young Doug, her son. It seems he was
in the ladies', though he swore he wasn't. One of the plain
clothes men said they'd found his fingerprints
everywhere. Personally, I don't believe it. He's not much
good as a worker, but he was very fond of his mother, and
Dora was devoted to him. We used to tease her about it.
Say he wasn't worth it, and that sort of thing.' Roberts
stopped suddenly, thinking that perhaps he'd said too
much. 'Was there something you wanted, sir?'

'Yes. I really came to ask if you'd seen Mr Terry Dale
this morning, if he's still in the club.'

'He's not, sir. Both Mr Dales left together, soon after
eight.'

'So early?' It was an involuntary remark. Gerald was
surprised. Terry had been very much the worse for wear
last night. In all fairness he should have suffered as much

as Gerald himself had; but it seemed he'd managed to emerge from drunken sleep in time to leave more than two hours ago.

'I see,' said Gerald. 'Thanks.' Sorting through a handful of change, he made his way to the phone-box that stood in a corner of the hall, disguised as a sedan chair. It was easier to ring Terry Dale from here than to go back to his room and put the call through the club switchboard. He found the number in his diary and dialled the advertising agency for which Terry Dale worked. A telephonist and two secretaries later he heard Terry's voice.

'Terry Dale speaking.' The voice was curt and business-like.

'Hi, Terry. It's Gerald Hinton. You're in good form after last night. How did you manage it?'

'Practice, old man, just practice. Anyway, I'm pretty busy this morning, and I just had to get in to the office.'

'I won't keep you, but I'm hoping you can help me.'

'Sure. How?'

'You remember the girl who burst into the party last night — Sally-Ann Belmont?'

There was a short pause, then: 'Who could forget? What — what about her?'

'Look, I think she's an actress of some kind — at least she's appeared in a TV ad. Do you remember that thing for chocolates a few years ago — "Give your golden girl a box of Gold" — it was quite well known in the trade, I'm sure. Now, I want you to help me trace her, Terry. I need to find her. I've got to prove to Elizabeth and her family that what the Belmont girl said was a bunch of lies.'

Gerald waited, but there was no reply. 'Terry! Terry, are you there?'

'Yes.'

It was a strangled monosyllable, and again Gerald waited. Finally he said, 'Terry! Are you all right?'

'I'm okay.' To Gerald he now sounded angry. 'I may sound fine, but in fact I've got a bit of a head. Not to be wondered at after that party, as you say. But about this Sally-Ann. Are you telling me that she really wasn't one of your ex-lays?'

'That's just what I'm saying!' It was Gerald's turn to be sharp. 'Terry, for God's sake, you didn't believe all that nonsense, did you?'

'Sorry, old boy. Sorry. I'll have to think. I'll have to check. I'll call you back in half an hour or so. You're still at the club?'

'Yes. Okay. Thanks, Terry. I'll wait for your call.'

Gerald told the porter he'd be in the Coffee Room, and went in search of a quiet chair where he could snooze unnoticed until the call came through.

When the porter summoned him, Gerald found it was a woman's voice on the line, prim and precise. She identified herself as Mr Dale's secretary. Mr Dale was in conference, but she had the information Mr Hinton required.

'You have? Splendid!' Gerald said.

'Do you have a pencil, Mr Hinton?'

There was always a pad beside the phone, and a pen on a long chain. 'Yes. Go ahead.'

'Well, that chocolate commercial with the golden girl theme wasn't one of ours, but we did employ Miss Sally-Ann Belmont about eighteen months ago. It was a short series of spots for a perfume company.'

'Fine,' said Gerald. 'But do you have an address for her, a phone number?'

'A home address? No. And if we did, we couldn't give it out, Mr Hinton. That would be quite contrary to the firm's policy.' The secretary sounded positively shocked at the idea, and Gerald gritted his teeth.

'But you must have some way of getting in touch with her. Suppose you wanted to use her again?'

'I was coming to that, Mr Hinton.' The voice sounded more precise than ever. 'Almost all our dealings with talent are through agents, and we naturally have the name and address of Miss Belmont's. That we can give you.'

'Thank you,' Gerald said with an attempt at meekness.

He took down what she dictated, read it back to her, thanked her, asked her to thank Mr Dale, and put down the receiver. The name and address on the pad in front of him were apparently those of a theatrical agency, and he hesitated about phoning it. He suspected he would meet the same professional reticence about the address of one of their clients. No. Some persuasion would be needed, and for that a personal approach would be infinitely better than a phone call.

Gerald was unused to such offices and found the premises of the Kalman Theatrical Agency pretty unimpressive — two rather dingy, cramped rooms on the top floor of a narrow and somewhat decrepit building off Shaftesbury Avenue. The walls were covered with signed photographs of the famous, the once-famous and the not-so-famous. Gerald looked hopefully for a picture of Sally-Ann Belmont, but was disappointed.

'And what can I do for you, Mr Hinton?' David Kalman leant across his desk and offered Gerald a slim, neatly-manicured hand.

Gerald shook it, and sat down in the chair that was indicated. He had expected difficulty in getting in to see Mr Kalman without an appointment; at least he had been prepared for a long wait. In fact, the two girls in the outer office had greeted him with a kind of amused interest, and there had been almost no delay before he was ushered into the second room. It crossed Gerald's mind that he might almost have been expected, but he dismissed the idea as absurd.

Gerald said, 'I won't waste your time, Mr Kalman. I'm trying to get in touch with a Miss Sally-Ann Belmont, and I'm told you might be able to help me. I believe you're her agent.'

David Kalman's smile was expansive, but perhaps a little guarded. 'I'm sorry, Mr Hinton, but I'm afraid your information's out of date. I was Miss Belmont's agent, but no more.'

'You mean she's changed to someone else? Who?'

'No. I mean she's not working now. She's given up the modelling and TV work she used to do. I heard she was thinking of getting herself married.'

'Did you? Where? I mean, where did you hear that?'

Kalman shrugged. 'I don't know. At some party or other, I think. Does it matter?'

'No.' Gerald moved restlessly in his chair. 'I take it you've still got an address for her.'

'I'm sorry, but no. The last time I called to offer her a job, she said she wasn't interested and told me to take her name off my books. So I did, and we've lost touch. That was months ago. I've no idea where she's living now.'

Kalman looked Gerald directly in the eye, and almost at once the telephone rang. It was too pat, Gerald thought, much too pat. He didn't believe Mr Kalman, but it was obvious he wasn't going to get any more from him. The interview was clearly at an end.

Kalman had picked up the receiver. 'Hello, darling. Lovely to hear from you. Yes, there's a nice little part coming up, just right for you. It's out of town to start with, but—' He put his hand over the mouthpiece. 'If you'll forgive me, Mr Hinton. An important client. Sorry I wasn't more help.'

'Don't mention it, Mr Kalman,' Gerald said drily. 'I'm grateful for your time.'

He let himself out of Kalman's room, walked past the girls, who again watched him with interest, and rang for the lift. He was at the front door of the building when he heard footsteps bounding down the stairs.

'Mr Hinton!'

Gerald turned. He recognized the boy at once from the tight green jeans and the orange shirt. He'd been leaning against a filing cabinet in a kind of open alcove off Kalman's outer office when Gerald first arrived, apparently doing nothing.

'Hey, Hinton, or whatever your name is. I heard you. I could help you, man — about the Belmont bird.'

'You? How?'

'See, if Kalman found out I was doing him dirt, I'd be in deep trouble. I don't fancy the dole.' The implication was obvious, even without the outstretched palm.

Gerald said nothing, but he took out his wallet. He had enough sense to turn away before he extracted two five pound notes. He turned back and held them between his fingers. The boy plucked them from him.

'I don't know where she's living or who she's shacking up with, but I do know she's got a bit part in one of the West End shows.'

'What? Now?'

'Sure.'

'Which one?'

'I'm not sure I remember.' The boy looked suggestively at the money he was holding.

There was nothing for it. Gerald produced another ten pounds. 'I suppose these will help. But it'd better be good.'

'Jeez, yes. Fine. She's in *Sirens on the Wind* at the Sheridan, just round the corner.'

'I know the place. But what kind of show is it? And how do I know you're telling me the truth?'

'Oh, for God's sake! Call the theatre. It's just a standard thriller. You know, coach parties from the sticks and all that. It's been running about six months.'

He was racing up the stairs before Gerald could ask any more questions. On the steps of the sleazy Soho building, Gerald paused in thought. He knew the theatre, if not the play. It was, as the boy had said, just around the corner. Three minutes later he was studying the prints in the showcases outside the Sheridan.

The boy hadn't lied. Almost immediately he found an excellent photograph of Sally-Ann Belmont in a group with the rest of the cast. She seemed to be playing some kind of waitress—not a leading role, but a part nevertheless. Yet she couldn't have been playing it the previous night.

For several minutes Gerald stared at the photograph. Then he went through the swing doors and across the foyer to the box office. As was inevitable, the one middle-aged woman on duty was on the phone, seemingly holding a complex negotiation with someone in a ticket agency. Finally, she hung up and turned to the wicket. Gerald asked politely if any seats were available for that evening.

'How many and how much?' asked the woman laconically. *Sirens on the Wind* might have been running for six months, but clearly it wasn't going to run much longer.

'Two stalls, preferably on a side aisle and near an exit.'

There was no problem. With the tickets in his pocket, Gerald went in search of a phone-box. Maybe he could get John Breland to go to the theatre that night.

CHAPTER 7

'That's the lot?' John Breland was scrubbing his hands at the basin in the corner of his consulting-room as Kathleen Taylor came in.

'That's all, Brel,' she said. 'Mrs Bristow was the last. Incidentally, it is Dr Farre who's taking calls over the weekend, isn't it?'

'Yes, Farre's the man,' replied Brel.

'Are you going out of town?'

'No,' Brel said. 'The first thing I've got to do is get down to the club as soon as possible. I promised the police superintendent I'd check and sign my statement about that wretched woman.'

'Her son seems to be the chief suspect.'

'What? How do you know?'

'It's all over the evening paper. A patient left a copy in the waiting-room and I snitched it. Front page news. "Murder at London Club. Body in Bath. Son Helps Police with Enquiries." That sort of thing. But it doesn't mention you.'

'That's something to be thankful for. I've a feeling the customers don't like to be reminded too often that doctors are mixed up with death.'

Brel took the paper that Kathleen was holding out to him, and skimmed the story. It said little more than the headlines, though it naturally made the most of the West End club angle. Brel noticed with interest that neither the broken vase nor the dagger in the display cabinet were mentioned. Clearly the police were keeping their own counsel about some aspects of the affair.

Kathleen said, 'I'm leaving now, Brel. I'll see you Monday morning.'

'Fine. Have a good weekend. I'm meeting Gerald Hinton at the club after I've dealt with the police, and we're going to the theatre. Then I'm having two quiet, uneventful days to myself.'

It took Brel twenty minutes to drive to the club through the early evening traffic, but he was lucky with parking. In the hall he met Alan Jenson.

'What a day, Dr Breland!' The secretary smiled resignedly. 'It's good to see you here. The Arts and Letters has become sort of "out of bounds", I think. Police everywhere — but members very scarce. And who can blame them? If it's not the police, it's the press. I hope you won't find them a nuisance.'

'They won't worry me, but it must be tough on you,' Brel said.

Jenson dismissed his own problems with a gesture. 'After all, it's part of my job to deal with emergencies.'

'Including murder?'

'I must admit it's not the kind of thing you expect.'

Brel had the impression that there was something the secretary wanted to say, but that he was finding it hard to put into words. 'Have there been any developments?' he prompted casually.

'I don't know. The police tell one nothing. Or very little.' Jenson hesitated. 'Have you seen the evening paper?'

'You mean about Doug Brown? Yes, I have.'

'I feel very badly about him. I had to dismiss him — he was careless and quite incompetent — and he's been a bother ever since. And one of the police officers let slip that he'd been in trouble before — he spent a year in a Borstal for knifing another boy. I had no idea when I took him on. You don't make detailed enquiries about casual help — and we knew his mother.'

'I see,' said Brel.

'Dr Breland, I know you've got to go and see the police, to make your statement. Do you think you could find out if they really suspect young Brown? For Dora's sake, I'd like to help him if it's necessary.'

Brel was a little nonplussed. Somehow he hadn't expected the club secretary to be so concerned about the likes of Doug Brown. 'I'll try,' he said at last. 'I'll do my best, but I doubt if they'll tell me much.'

In this Brel found he was wrong. Chief Superintendent Freeman was surprisingly forthcoming. Brel's statement duly checked and signed, Freeman expressed his gratitude.

'Very grateful for your help, Dr Breland. That was a good tip you gave us about the dagger in the display cabinet. We'd have got round to it sooner or later, I guess, but you saved us a lot of time.'

'It really was the weapon?'

'Almost certainly. It had been washed and hurriedly dried, but our lab found traces of blood — the same group as Mrs Brown's — in the carving around the handle.'

'No fingerprints, I suppose?'

'Not on the dagger. Plenty on the cabinet. We're still trying to sort them out. So, if you wouldn't mind, Doctor . . .'

Brel grinned. 'Not a bit. I did touch it, though only with my fingernail, to make sure it was unlocked. I don't think I left any mark.'

The fingerprinting took only a few seconds. Brel watched the process with interest, wondering how he could turn the conversation to Doug Brown. He said tentatively, 'Isn't it a bit odd, Chief Superintendent, that the dagger wasn't left in the body? Why should someone go to all the trouble of putting it back in the cabinet?'

'It is odd, yes,' the Chief Superintendent agreed, 'but we find people often behave irrationally after they've killed, especially if the murder was violent and unpremeditated.'

'Doug Brown?' said Brel.

A pair of amused shrewd eyes regarded him. 'Possibly, Doctor. Possibly. But I very much doubt it. His prints are on the service door and in the cloakroom itself. I'd guess that he tried to attract his mother's attention, as he said, and when he failed, he poked his head in, saw no one and had a quick look round for anything worth taking. But, unless he put gloves on specially, he didn't go into the dressing-room where the body was—the door was probably shut as Mrs Sencourt found it—or out into the little cul-de-sac where the dagger was. Anyway, we didn't find any of his dabs in either place.'

'And if he was going to wear gloves part of the time,' asked Brel, 'why didn't he put them on to start with?'

'Exactly,' said Freeman.

'So he's in the clear, in spite of the newspaper stories?'

The Chief Superintendent shrugged. 'Don't pay too much attention to the papers. But he could be cleverer than we think. He admits to having had a violent quarrel with his ma before she left for work. And he's got a bit of a record, though I shouldn't tell you that, I suppose. Besides, the only alternative theory we've come up with is that Dora Brown saw someone she recognized messing about with the display cabinet, and had to be killed—which is pretty far-fetched.' He grinned suddenly. 'Unless you've got any more bright ideas, Doctor?'

Brel returned the grin. 'Not at the moment, Chief Superintendent, but I'll work on it.'

'Terrific!' Mike Freeman said sardonically.

Half an hour later Brel was sitting with Gerald Hinton in a corner of the men's bar, one of the few remaining parts of the club to which women weren't admitted. The secretary had been right; they were the only members in the place. They were both drinking whisky, and Brel felt he needed his. His earlier moderate enthusiasm for the play they were to see had rapidly evaporated in the face of a more detailed understanding of just what Gerald had in mind.

'We'll go backstage after the show, and I'll wring the truth out of that Belmont bitch,' Gerald had said. He sounded determined and full of purpose.

Brel acquiesced doubtfully, and drained his glass. His own experience of Sally-Ann Belmont, both in his office and at the club, suggested that she was tough enough to withstand meaningless threats. She would only cooperate if it suited her, or could be made to seem to suit her. Gentle persuasion and explanation, assisted by a little quiet bribery, would appear to be indicated. Still, there was no point in trying to dissuade Gerald in his present mood.

But Brel did make one comment. 'What I can't understand is why you made no attempt to tackle the matter when you were at the theatre this morning. There was probably some manager on the premises, and you could have explained the situation to him. He could have been very interested to know why one of his actresses didn't appear last night. He might have given you her address.'

'I doubt it. That damned agent wouldn't. All these people stick together. No, this is the best way. They can't warn her, and I'll have you to back me up as a witness.'

Brel shook his head. 'The Lydneys may not accept me as unbiased, you know. Have you considered that?'

'Yes. I want her to sign a couple of sentences, saying the whole thing was a hoax and a joke. Then I'll be satisfied—for the moment. If it was Ryle who put her up to it—and the more I think about it, the more convinced I am it was—I'll deal with him later. I don't want to make a fuss, cause a lot of trouble between him and Elizabeth and the parents right now, just before the wedding.'

Brel nodded. He was becoming tired and a little bored with Gerald and his problems. He was thankful for the interruption of the barman, bringing them the pre-theatre sandwiches they had ordered.

'Sorry to be so long, gentlemen, but I'm short-handed tonight. Not that it matters much.' He glanced around the empty bar. 'Business is slack, even for a Friday, but the kitchen staff are a bit upset.'

'I'm not surprised,' said Brel. 'At least you seem to be free of police in here.'

'True enough, sir,' the barman acknowledged. 'Now, what else can I get you?'

'Two more whiskies,' Gerald said.

'That's what I need,' said Brel. But the brief conversation with the barman had reminded him of Alan Jenson's request concerning Doug Brown. As soon as he had eaten his sandwich and finished his drink he said to Gerald, 'I'll meet you in the hall in five minutes or so. We haven't got much time, but I'd like a word with the secretary if I can find him.'

'Sure. Try his office.'

But Jenson was not in his office and Brel, coming out of the cloakroom, met him only by chance. 'Ah!' he said. 'The man I'm looking for.'

'You've got some news, Doctor? You've seen the Superintendent?'

'Yes, I have. He was fairly noncommittal, but I don't think there's any need to worry about young Brown — not in the immediate future, anyway. I rather gathered that he's the prime suspect because they can't think of anyone else. There doesn't seem to be any real evidence against him.'

'Splendid! I'm so glad.' Alan Jenson's face lit up with pleasure. 'Thank you very much indeed, Dr Breland. That was very good of you. I could get nothing out of the police myself. I'm most grateful.'

Brel waved away the thanks, which seemed a little disproportionate to the effort he had expended. Gerald was waiting for him in the hall, and he didn't want to be late for the play. 'I must go,' he said. 'Mr Hinton and I are just off to see *Sirens on the Wind.*'

'*Sirens on the Wind?*' The secretary sounded surprised.

'Yes. Have you seen it?'

'Actually I have, yes. Sir Richard Wander was good

enough to give me a ticket. I think he's got an investment in the play. He's very keen on the theatre. His wife was an actress, as I'm sure you know, Doctor.'

'Really?'

It crossed Brel's mind that the club secretary knew a great deal about the members' private affairs, probably more than most of them suspected, but he said good night affably enough. He found an impatient Gerald in the hall.

'Where have you been? We'll have to hurry. It's not worth taking the car or a cab, but it's a fair step to the Sheridan.'

In the event they arrived at the theatre in good time. The one minute bell had just sounded, the bar was emptying fast, the usherettes were ready to close the doors and draw the curtains. Gerald bought two programmes, shook his head at the offer of sweets or chocolates and allowed Brel and himself to be shown to their seats. At once he thrust a programme at Brel, and opened his own.

'There!' he said triumphantly. 'Found her!' He stabbed a finger at the cast list. 'Nina — Sally-Ann Belmont.' He riffled through the pages, but apparently her part was too small to justify an individual photograph or any notes on her career. She could, however, be seen in the background of an action shot of a scene from the play.

Gerald turned to Brel. 'That's good, eh? Now we're really getting somewhere.'

Brel barely caught the words. His interest was concentrated on his surroundings. It was a gem of a theatre, and he was admiring the gilded angels supporting one of the boxes when he stiffened. A man was sitting towards the rear of the box — perhaps a public figure who preferred not to be recognized. The man suddenly leant forward. Peter Dale? Brel wasn't absolutely sure, but it was very like him. An odd coincidence, if it were Peter.

Brel turned towards Gerald, but at that moment the house lights dimmed and a man in a dinner-jacket slipped between the heavy crimson tabs. He stood at the front of the apron, bathed in a spot.

'Ladies and gentlemen,' he said, 'I have a brief announcement. Unfortunately Miss Sally-Ann Belmont is indisposed. The part of Nina will be played by Miss Joan Grey. We beg your indulgence. Thank you.'

The man stepped back and the spotlight faded. There was no noticeable reaction from the audience. After all, Sally-Ann Belmont was hardly one of the stars they had come to see. The curtain rose to reveal the set — the interior of a Mediterranean café, with a view of the sea beyond.

Gerald gripped Brel's arm. 'Did you hear that? She's not here. She's ill.'

'Sure I heard, but I doubt if she's ill. She certainly wasn't ill last night.'

'But what shall we do?'

'Sh-u-sh!' A hushing sound came from behind them, and the couple in front turned round and gave them a reproachful glare. Gerald subsided. Brel waited until a ripple of applause greeted the entrance of the leading man — an actor well-known from his television appearances. Then he leaned towards Gerald, and whispered, 'Let's think a bit. At least wait for the interval. Maybe we can tackle the theatre manager then.'

Brel was wondering whether in fact the theatre authorities would be prepared to divulge any useful information to a couple of random enquirers. If not, he thought, he might use the name of Sir Richard Wander as a lever of some kind. In the meantime he tried to concentrate on the play. Gerald, fidgeting in the seat beside him, didn't help.

The curtain came down and the house lights rose. With one accord, Gerald and Brel made straight for the bar at the back of the stalls. At least, thought Brel, a half empty house made it easier to get a drink.

As he was moving away from the bar Brel noticed the dinner-jacketed man who had made the announcement about Sally-Ann Belmont standing beside an unmarked door in a corner of the room. He nudged Gerald, and together they approached him.

'Good evening,' Brel said. 'I wonder if we could speak to whoever's in charge of the theatre.'

'If you've got a complaint or you want to change your seats, I'm the FOH manager on duty tonight. What's the problem?' The man spoke pleasantly, with a slight Transatlantic accent.

'FOH?' queried Brel.

'Front of house. I look after the customers. They look after the show.' He jerked his thumb in the direction of the stage.

'But you made the announcement about Miss Belmont.'

'That's because I'm the only guy in the place in a tuxedo. They called me from backstage. It happens now and then.'

'You may be able to help us all the same. It's about Miss Belmont. We want her address.'

'Oh you do, do you? Who are you? Creditors?'

Brel laughed. 'Nothing like that. It's a personal matter.'

'Personal, eh.' He looked at Brel and Gerald appraisingly. 'Well, I couldn't give out that information without authority. You could write to Miss Belmont care of the theatre, or I could possibly find her agent's name.'

'It's a lot more urgent than that,' said Gerald. 'In fact, it's a matter of real importance.'

'Is it now?' The man hesitated. 'Well, see here, gentlemen, you look pretty respectable to me, so I'll level with you. Officially I don't know a thing about Miss

Belmont except that she didn't turn up last night, and she wasn't playing tonight. Unofficially I don't mind telling you she phoned yesterday to say she was ill. Fair enough?'

'Fair enough,' said Brel. 'Thanks a lot.'

'Oh, there's more. I know what I'd do if I was in your shoes and wanted to get hold of Miss Belmont urgently. I'd wait till after the show, then go round behind and try and get the stage-door keeper to let me have a word with June Clairvale. She dresses with her.'

'She does what?' said Brel.

'Dresses with her—shares a dressing-room with the Belmont girl.'

'I understand,' said Brel. 'We're most grateful.'

The manager grinned. 'Forget it,' he said. 'There's the bell. Enjoy the play.' He opened the door of his office.

Somewhat reluctantly Gerald allowed himself to be led back into the auditorium. As they settled into their seats and before the house lights dimmed, Brel glanced up at the box in which he thought he'd seen Peter Dale. It was empty now, nor had there been any sign of Peter in the bar. Clearly, if it had been Peter, he'd not bothered to wait for the second act.

The second act was a little more exciting than the first, but Gerald was more restless. As soon as the final curtain began to fall, he was standing up.

'Come on,' he said to Brel. 'Let's go.'

'There's no hurry,' said Brel. 'It'll take them a few minutes to change.'

Gerald paid no attention. He led the way through the foyer and out of the theatre, looking to right and left. 'If we follow the block round this way, we must get to the Stage Door,' he said. Brel followed without protest, around a corner and along an ill-lit cobbled alley. At the end was an entrance with a light over it. Gerald pushed open a swing door and started down the passage inside.

'Hey! Where do you think you're going?' A voice emerged from a lighted cubicle on the right. It reminded Brel somewhat of an untidy version of the porter's box at the Arts and Letters.

'We want to see Miss Clairvale,' said Gerald curtly.

'Is she expecting you?'

'No. You just point her out to us.' Gerald took out his wallet.

Surprisingly it was quite the wrong approach. 'Now look here,' said the stage-door keeper, 'we don't do things like that around here. You'd better get out. I can't stop you waiting in the alley.'

Brel intervened quickly. 'It's all right,' he said. 'It's not like that. Just tell her we want to speak to her about Miss Belmont.'

'You're friends of Miss Belmont's?' asked the man suspiciously.

'More or less,' said Brel. 'I'm her doctor. Just tell Miss Clairvale that.'

The door keeper's suspicions were apparently easily allayed. 'Oh, that's different,' he said at once. 'Why didn't you say so in the first place. Anyway, that's June Clairvale there. Miss Clairvale,' he called. 'There's two gentlemen here asking for you.'

A girl in her late twenties, whom Brel recognized as a minor character in the play, was sweeping past them with a cheerful, ' 'Night, Trevor.' She paused.

'Yes?' she said quite pleasantly. She was small and dark with a pert face, an upturned nose and bright, intelligent eyes. Brel decided she wouldn't be easily fooled.

'I'm Dr John Breland, Miss Clairvale,' he said, 'and this is Mr Hinton. We need to get in touch with Sally-Ann Belmont.'

'I can't help you.'

'Will you let us explain? It really is desperately important.' As she looked swiftly from Gerald to himself, he added, 'Is there somewhere round here where we could have a drink together and tell you about it? Please.'

June Clairvale hesitated, but Brel could be very persuasive. The clefts in his cheeks deepened as he smiled at her, and she caught herself looking at him speculatively for a moment. 'Okay,' she said. 'The pubs'll be shutting soon, but there's a club most of us belong to round the corner.'

They said good-night again to Trevor, who nodded approvingly; apparently the arrangements met with his satisfaction. They walked back down the cobbled alley, crossed a couple of narrow streets and quickly found themselves at the top of some steps down to the basement of a nondescript building.

The club — it had no name that Brel ever discovered — was very efficient. A nod from Miss Clairvale to a large man behind a desk in yet another porter's booth saved Brel and Gerald from any 'entrance fee', a mynah bird seated on a perch beside a long bar said 'good evening' politely and was apparently unsurprised to receive no sensible reply, a table was quickly found for them and drinks ordered. It was a cheerful, relaxing place. An accordion was playing in the background and two or three couples revolved in tight embraces on a minute dance floor.

'This is fun,' said Brel in genuine appreciation.

June Clairvale looked at him. 'Sure,' she replied. 'There's got to be some way of avoiding the licensing laws. Now, what's all this about Sally-Ann?'

Gerald was about to speak, but Brel put a hand on his arm. This was a moment for tact, a trait that Gerald seemed to lack this evening.

'Look, Miss Clairvale,' said Brel. 'it's like this . . .'

He gave June Clairvale a slightly expurgated account of what he described as the hoax that had been played on

Gerald. He showed every sympathy with it as a stag party gag, but emphasized the special circumstances which could make its consequences particularly unfortunate. '. . . Surely Miss Belmont wouldn't really want to break up a serious engagement for the sake of a joke,' he concluded.

June Clairvale listened earnestly, but when he had finished she shook her head. 'I believe you, every word. I wish I could help but I can't.'

'But I must find her,' Gerald said desperately. 'I must. All I want is an address or a phone number—quickly, now, tonight. Don't you understand?'

'Sure, of course. I said I'd help if I could. But I don't know where she is. Sally-Ann shared a flat with me for a couple of months after *Sirens* came into town. Then one day she moved out. It was wretchedly inconvenient, and I've had a hell of a job paying the rent since she left. But she said her boy-friend was setting her up in a swish apartment in Chelsea. As soon as *Sirens* folded they were going to get married. What could I say? What could I do? Let's face it, she wasn't the world's greatest actress—even bit-part actress—and her boy-friend seemed to have plenty of cash. You should see some of the presents he gave her.'

'Did she ever take you to see this new apartment?' Brel asked.

'No. And I didn't expect her to. She was an odd girl. Secretive. She never told me where it was exactly, or who the man was. We weren't really what I'd call friends. We shared for convenience. That's all.'

'But what was his first name?' Brel said. 'The boyfriend's? She must have called him something.'

'You've got a point there. She always referred to him as "my boy-friend", and I never askd. On the phone it was always "love" or "darling" or something, though I think she once did say "Gerry".'

'But that's absurd,' Gerald burst out. 'It can't be. It's my name. At least, Gerald is.'

June Clairvale laughed. 'Got a monopoly?' she said.

'No. No, I suppose not.' Gerald seemed surprisingly upset. He stood up. 'If you'll excuse me a minute.'

He set off, a little unsteadily in the direction of the gents' cloakroom, and June Clairvale stared after him. She turned to Brel. 'Strange guy,' she said. Then she paused as a thought struck her, and suddenly was belligerent. 'You're not having me on about all this, are you?'

'No, no,' said Brel gently. 'No. It's all above board.'

At least, I hope so, he added to himself.

CHAPTER 8

The doorbell rang as Brel was having breakfast. Cursing, he went to the intercom. Someone had probably pushed the wrong button. Either they wanted the housekeeper, who lived in the basement flat, or the dentist who had rooms on the ground floor and sometimes saw patients on a Saturday. Or someone had merely got the wrong house.

'Yes? Who do you want?'

'Brel, it's Gerald.'

John Breland contained himself with difficulty. 'Oh, good morning. Come on up.' He pressed the button that released the front door lock. Brel knew he didn't sound particularly welcoming but who, he thought, could blame him. He'd really had his fill of Gerald and Gerald's problems. As he saw it, if Elizabeth Lydney was not prepared to accept Gerald's word about his relation-ship — or lack of it — with Sally-Ann Belmont, then Gerald was better off not marrying her. But it was impossible to state this obvious fact so bluntly.

Sighing, Brel opened the door of his flat. 'Hello, Gerald,' he said. 'I thought you'd be on the way to spend the weekend with the Lydneys.'

'I was. I am — if you'll do something for me.'

'What?'

Gerald followed Brel into the sitting-room. 'I was leaving the club just now when Roberts, the porter, gave me this. He said the maid had found it in a corner of my room, under the bed. She pulled the bed out to put on clean sheets.'

Brel took the thin gold evening bag that Gerald held out to him, and opened it. It contained some minimum make-up, a handkerchief, a couple of Yale-type keys — and a wallet. There were twenty-two pounds in the wallet, and a few credit cards. One of the credit cards, from a major London department store, had the name and address of the owner embossed on the plastic.

'Sally-Ann Belmont!' Brel exclaimed. 'Well, now you know where she lives. But what did you say? To Roberts, I mean? I hope you denied all knowledge of the bag — and of Sally-Ann Belmont.'

'No. How could I, when it was found under my bed?'

'Oh, Gerald —' Brel shook his head in disbelief. 'If it's nothing to do with you, you should have said so at once. You should have refused to take the bag. You're just getting yourself more and more involved.'

'That's not my fault. Roberts already knows — believes — she's a friend of mine. Look at all those phone calls to the club. She kept asking for me, and finally gave her name, remember?' Gerald's words tripped over each other in his anxiety to explain. 'Don't you understand? There was no point in trying to tell him anything. I just took the bag — and a good thing too. As you say, we've got her address.'

'And you're proposing to go round there, return the bag, and confront—'

'No. That's the point. I can't. I must get to the Lydneys' on time. Elizabeth's father's a stickler for punctuality. And coming here's made me late already.'

'But, Gerald, this is a good sight more important than getting down to Kent. If you can arrive there with an explanation—'

'That's not the only thing. I'm not sure it'd be a good idea for me to go myself. I shouldn't be able to swear the only time I ever saw the Belmont girl was at that wretched party. No. You've just got to go for me. Please, Brel!'

' "Got to," nothing! That's asking too much.' Brel didn't know whether to be amused or exasperated. What had started as a rather unpleasant hoax seemed to be getting completely out of hand. Even if there had been a serious intention to prevent Gerald's marrage, this fresh incident remained inexplicable. Yet another effort to incriminate Gerald—or at least to compromise him—by planting the bag under his bed was surely gilding the lily.

'Brel, please. I must get down there and see Elizabeth. I don't trust Lydney or Ryle. She'll understand, I'm sure. Probably I should have gone yesterday, but they weren't expecting me, and I hoped I could find Sally-Ann . . .'

Gerald's voice trailed hopelessly away. His usually robust face was white and puffy from lack of sleep, and he seemed utterly miserable. Against his will, Brel relented.

'All right, damn you!' He grinned, making an effort to be cheerful. 'You've ruined my morning, but I'll forgive you. Get going, then. But if her current boy-friend's at home and turns out to be a heavyweight boxer, I'll hold you responsible.' It was a meaningless remark, but it seemed to calm Gerald.'

'And you'll phone me tonight at the Lydneys',' he said. 'Yes.'

'Thanks, Brel. I can't tell you how grateful I am.'

'I'll do what I can. Now, get going.'

Finding Miss Belmont's address proved more difficult
than Brel had expected, and it was only with the help of a
friendly postman that he managed to locate it off the
Fulham Road. Geographically, it could hardly be called
Chelsea, but the block of flats in which Miss Belmont
lived looked both attractive and expensive. Freshly
painted, its window-boxes full of flowers, small trees in
tubs on either side of the steps to the entrance, it even had
a certain elegance. One thing it seemed to lack, however,
was a porter or doorman.

Instead, inside the outer double doors, it had a modern
secure entry control system, with a telephone-type keypad
in place of the usual selection of separate bells, and no list
of tenants. Brel took Sally-Ann's bag from his pocket and
found the number of her apartment — 42 — on the credit
card. As he tapped it out and waited, he thought that
whoever paid the rent must write a handsome cheque
each month. There was no answer, no voice from the
small loudspeaker beside the keypad, no welcoming click
from the inner door lock. Nor was there any indication of
the presence of a resident housekeeper whom he might
consult. Brel tried again, without result. Loath to depart
without accomplishing anything at all — even the return
of the bag to its owner — he was hesitating about trying
one or other of Miss Belmont's keys on the inner door,
when it opened and a woman emerged, carrying a
shopping-bag.

'Good morning,' she said brightly. 'Lovely day, isn't it?'

'Lovely,' Brel agreed. The woman was holding the
inner door open for him and, almost without thinking, he
walked past her into a small, carpeted hall. 'Thanks very
much,' he said over his shoulder, reflecting that even the
best security systems failed to cope with personal
politeness.

The door shut itself automatically behind him. In an alcove on his right Brel saw two rows of metal mailboxes, each bearing a number but no name. The slit in each box would take a small note, but certainly not an evening bag; obviously the postman opened the whole front of the installation with a master key in order to distribute the mail. Neither of Sally-Ann's keys would fit her box.

Directly opposite was a lift, and beside it a staircase led upwards. Brel took the stairs, and found Miss Belmont's apartment at the end of a corridor on the fourth floor. He pressed the bell, keeping his thumb firmly on it, and could hear the angry buzzing inside. But again there was no response. She could be fast asleep, he supposed, but it was much more likely that she was out or away for the weekend.

The door of the flat had no slot for letters, through which he might have pushed the bag. In the circumstances, he was reluctant to involve Miss Belmont's neighbours. So, either he departed, even the least part of his mission — the return of the bag — unaccomplished, or he let himself into the flat with one of Miss Belmont's keys.

The first key didn't work. Brel tried the second and the door opened. As he pushed against it he took a step into the hall of the flat, and in that moment his mind photographed the scene before him — the oriental rug, the bowl of roses on an ornately carved table, the oval mirror on the wall above the table and, reflected in the mirror, the man pressing himself back behind the door in a seemingly desperate effort to avoid being seen.

Instinctively Brel thrust harder at the door, pinning the man against the wall. There was a muffled shout, half pain, half anger. Brel released the pressure. And, at the same moment, something struck him hard behind his left ear. His legs crumpled and he pitched forward. He wasn't conscious of hitting the floor.

★

Brel opened his eyes slowly and found himself looking up at a blue-painted ceiling. He was lying on his back, which at once struck him as odd, and someone had loosened his tie and undone the top button of his shirt. At least they didn't mean me to choke, he thought wryly, as he gently felt his skull behind the ear. He winced as his fingers probed, and damned his attacker.

It was quite pleasant lying there. The carpet was thick, and the view of ceiling and carved table legs not uninteresting. He looked at his watch; he couldn't have been unconscious for more than three or four minutes. Then he stiffened as he saw the gold evening bag open on the floor beside him, its contents scattered. Gently Brel raised himself on one elbow, then got to his feet. He didn't hurry. He was sure by now that he was alone in the flat, and like most doctors he took his own physical ailments very seriously.

He collected the contents of the bag. They were intact, and the money and credit cards were still in the wallet. As he knew, he hadn't disturbed any ordinary thieves. He added the keys that had fallen to the floor, and placed the bag on the hall table. He told himself he should leave at once, but curiosity was strong.

He walked slowly down the passage. All the doors stood open, and after glancing through the first — into a good-sized, living-room — he moved very warily, and was careful with his hands. The flat, though luxuriously furnished, was small, with but one bedroom, a bathroom and a kitchen, and Brel was soon back in the hall. Then he took out his handkerchief, wiped the surface of the table and anything else he might have touched and went through the evening bag, polishing every article it contained. His fingerprints, after all, were now on the police files, and he had no wish to be accused of rifling Sally-Ann Belmont's flat.

For someone had been through it with a fine-tooth comb. Each room had been thoroughly searched. Cupboards were open, clothes emptied from drawers, pictures askew, cushions on sofa and chairs disarranged. No attempt had been made to disguise the intrusion. Miss Belmont would not be pleased, Brel thought.

Keeping his handkerchief around his hand, Brel opened the flat door a careful inch. There was no sound outside and no one to be seen in the corridor. Quickly he slipped through the door, polished the outer handle and the area around the lock and walked down the stairs. He met no one. He let himself out of the building and made for his car.

For a full minute he sat behind the steering-wheel, doing nothing. From one point of view he could laugh at what had happened, and be amused at his amateur efforts to behave like a minor criminal, but his overriding feeling was anger. The blow behind his ear had been no joke.

He felt the place tenderly again. No longer was the problem of Sally-Ann Belmont Gerald's alone. Now it had become personal, and Brel was determined to take action himself. What was more, he had a good idea where to start. He didn't know who had hit him, though he could make a guess, but the attack had not been quick enough, nor had the man behind the door moved quickly enough to prevent Brel's identification of his reflection.

CHAPTER 9

Brel was surprised to find that it was only just after eleven o'clock when he got back home to Harley Street. The morning had been so full of incident it already seemed like lunch-time—not that he felt much like eating. He made himself a mug of instant coffee and went into the bathroom to juggle with mirrors in an attempt to examine the dully aching bump behind his ear. It was already turning blue, but the skin was only slightly grazed and he had no signs or symptoms of any serious injury.

His first objective was to locate Terry Dale. He lifted the phone and dialled. Jennifer Dale answered, and in her high-pitched, piercing voice explained that Terry was not at home. He and Peter had been stupid enough to agree to a police request that they should drive up to London on a Saturday morning to check their statements about that cloakroom attendant who had got herself killed at the Arts and Letters. 'As if they had anything to do with it,' she ended fiercely.

'Quite,' Brel agreed noncommittally. 'When do you expect Terry back?'

'By twelve-thirty at the latest. They promised faithfully, police or no police. I've twenty people coming to lunch at one, and I told them both they'd got to be here at least half an hour before.'

'Quite,' Brel said again, feeling a momentary pang of sympathy for the Dale brothers, and especially for Jennifer Dale's husband. 'Thank you very much. I'm sorry to have bothered you.'

Brel put his receiver down quickly, before Jennifer could launch into another tirade. Then he called the Arts and Letters. It was possible, he thought, that they might be at the club — a good guess, as it turned out.

'Yes, Dr Breland,' Roberts said. 'Both Mr Dales came in a few minutes ago. They're in the Coffee Room. I'll call Mr Terry.'

'Thanks.'

Brel waited. His anger had subsided a little, but his mood was still grim, and it annoyed him that Peter, not Terry, should come to the phone.

'Hello, Brel. Peter here. How are you?'

'No better for being coshed.'

'Coshed?'

'Yes, coshed. Don't play the bloody innocent, Peter. And listen to me. I'm coming down to the club right now to talk to Terry—and you. I'll expect you both to be there.'

'But my dear chap, that's not possible. We've got to get home. Terry's just gone to fetch the car. Jenny's giving one of her lunch parties, and there'll be hell to pay if the family aren't all there on time.'

'Peter, even more hell will break loose if I have to tell Jennifer what her beloved Terry's been doing with Sally-Ann Belmont.'

'Oh, for Christ's sake, Brel! Listen—'

Brel was getting angry. 'For Christ's sake, nothing. You just wait there, both of you. I'm fully prepared to listen. In fact, that's what I want to do—listen to the whole bloody truth—unexpurgated. It'll be a waste of time for you and Terry to try and concoct some fancy story. I know too much already. So just wait. I'll be with you in a few minutes.'

Without giving Peter Dale a chance to reply, Brel slammed down the receiver. If the noise damaged Peter's eardrum, he was glad. For it was Terry Dale whom he had seen trying to flatten himself against the wall behind the door in Sally-Ann Belmont's flat that morning. And it was common knowledge that Peter was always ready at hand when Terry got himself into any trouble. He was prepared to bet that Peter had been the other man in the flat, who'd slugged him.

Again he was lucky with parking, and twenty minutes later he found himself smiling sourly at the elder of the two Dale brothers, waiting for him in the entrance lobby of the club.

'Terry's still here?' he asked abruptly.

'Yes, indeed, Brel. We've found a nice quiet corner in

the drawing-room where we can talk without being disturbed — and get a drink when the bar opens.'

Peter grinned ingratiatingly, but Brel made no reply. As was only to be expected, his head was still aching, and he saw no reason to be pleasant to the Dales. As soon as he reached the drawing-room, he flung himself into an armchair directly opposite Terry and, without preamble, said, 'Well, get on with it. Tell me about Sally-Ann Belmont — the whole truth, remember.'

'Why the hell should I?' Terry Dale made an attempt at belligerence. 'It's none of your damn business, Brel.'

'You'd prefer to explain to your wife?'

'No, but — Anyway, what about you?'

'Me? I haven't got a wife.'

'I know that. I'm talking about your medical ethics. Wouldn't your Medical Council or whatever it's called like to know about you and one of your patients?'

Brel looked at Terry in disgust. 'Are you suggesting I've been having an affair with Miss Belmont?'

'Why not? You had a key to her flat.'

'I don't need to explain to you, but I was returning the evening bag she left at the club on Thursday. The key was in it. When no one answered the doorbell, I let myself in. I didn't expect to be assaulted.' He turned to Peter as Terry began to expostulate.

Peter said quickly, 'Shut up, Terry. Look, I'm sorry about that, Brel. You surprised us. We didn't want to be caught in there and I — I just grabbed a paperweight or something from the table in the hall and hit out. I hadn't even recognized you when I did it.'

'If you'd recognized me you wouldn't have hit so hard, I suppose,' Brel said caustically.

Peter Dale shrugged. 'I've apologized. What more do you want? Luckily there was no harm done. And I've told Terry he's got to explain.'

'Then I suggest he starts, instead of wasting time

making bloody stupid accusations.'

'All right, all right,' Terry said, resigned at last. 'I met her—Sally-Ann—at the beginning of last winter. I was looking for a girl for a two-minute commercial spot. We needed a blonde and David Kalman—her agent—sent her round to the office. Okay, if you must know, I fell for her, just like that. I was rather flush at the time and a few months later, when a chap I know wanted to sublet his flat while he spent a couple of years in the States, I set her up in it.'

For a moment, remembering, he lapsed into silence. Then, heaving a sigh, he went on. 'It was fine for a while, but then she began to get ideas. She started to talk about marriage and me getting a divorce. She said she loved me and she wanted to settle down and have kids. Hell! I've already got kids, three of them, and in the long run I couldn't bear to part from them. Come to that, I couldn't part from Jenny either. She'd take me for every penny I've got—not that most of it isn't her money—and she'd turn the kids against me. I knew all that, I suppose, but I was so bloody scared of losing Sally-Ann, I played along—strung her along . . .'

He paused again, looking restlessly around him. 'God!' he said. 'I need a drink. When's that bar going to open? Peter!'

Peter went in search of drinks and Terry continued, hurriedly, almost as if he were now glad to tell the story. 'The next thing, the bitch was pregnant. She admitted she'd done it on purpose to force my hand, and she laughed when I mentioned abortion. She said it was too late, and in any case she wanted the child. She threatened to tell Jenny, if I didn't tell her first. I thought my goose was cooked. Then Gerald gave that party—'

He stopped abruptly. Peter had reappeared, followed by a very youthful-looking barman carrying a tray of whiskies and a siphon. Terry took his drink straight, and had drained it before Peter had paid.

'The same again — all round,' Terry said.

'V — very good, sir.' The barman stuttered slightly.

Brel waited till he was out of earshot. Then he prompted, 'So — Gerald's party?'

Terry stared at him in surprise. 'Well, Sally-Ann told the world who was really the father. Gerald, of course. You heard her. She accused him in front of everyone. I was flabbergasted when she appeared — and at what she said. But it solved my problem.'

'She was pretty disconcerted too,' Peter put in. 'She had no idea Terry was going to be there. Didn't you see how she sort of faltered when she saw him and then recovered herself?'

Brel nodded. He had noticed Sally-Ann Belmont's sudden hesitation, just as he'd seen Terry Dale's stunned expression — and Nick Ryle's amusement.

Brel said quietly, 'Gerald denies the whole thing.'

'He would, wouldn't he?' said Peter.

'I believe him, for one,' Brel said.

'Would you bet your life on it?'

'I don't give a damn who believes who,' Terry interrupted, 'as long as there's enough doubt for Jenny. She'll raise hell, but she'll forgive me in the end if she thinks it was just another affair. She always has in the past, and she knows I'm not the most faithful of husbands. It's the child and the prospect of divorce that would have made it look so serious. But that's all over. Someone else has been accused of being the father — and we've got my letters back.' Terry grinned triumphantly.

'I see,' said Brel. The arrival of the barman with the second round of drinks intervened. When the man had gone he said simply, as if it weren't the first time he'd heard of any letters, 'Did they mention the child?'

'Yes. Once or twice. And in one of them I promised to divorce Jenny. I was abroad at the time, and missing

Sally-Ann like hell. If Jenny saw those letters, she'd never forgive me. And I wouldn't expect her to, either,' he added surprisingly. 'Anyway, now there's nothing on paper to show it was at all serious—it's only Sally-Ann's word against mine. If Jenny does get to hear about all this—and I hope to God she doesn't—it won't seem any different from the other times.' Terry stopped, and looked hopefully at Brel.

'Okay, Terry. Your wife won't hear of it from me, but when Sally-Ann finds the letters gone she'll know who ransacked her flat. She won't feel very charitable towards you. Why did you make such a hell of a mess?'

'They were well hidden, and we'd only just got them when you appeared,' said Peter. 'We didn't want to hang around till you woke up.'

'How did you know I was ever going to wake up?' said Brel bitterly. 'Blows on the head . . .'

There was a pause while they drank. Then Peter said. 'Okay, okay, Brel. I've said I'm sorry. But look, just assume for a moment that Terry's right and Gerald really is the father. Why do you think Sally-Ann made that scene at the party—to spite him because he's denied it? I can't believe it was only a hoax. It was altogether too vicious and complicated.'

'God knows.' Brel finished his whisky and stood up. He'd had enough of the Dale brothers for one morning, and he didn't want to discuss Gerald with them. 'Thanks for the drinks. Incidentally, I suppose you don't know where Sally-Ann is, do you?'

'No. I guess she's gone away for the weekend—probably with some other guy,' Peter said. 'We tried to find her yesterday. After the business with Gerald, we hoped she'd be prepared to give Terry his letters back, in return for some kind of golden handshake, perhaps. It was only when we found she still wasn't home this morning that we decided to go in and grab them.'

'Peter even went to the Sheridan last night to try and make contact. She's got a part in a play there — *Sirens* — '

'I know. I saw him. Gerald and I were there. We wanted to see her too.'

'You were? I didn't see you.' Peter frowned somewhat suspiciously. 'But then I didn't stay very long once I'd heard the announcement.'

'How did you find out where she was playing?' Terry asked. 'Her agent, I suppose. I asked Kalman not to tell Gerald she was in a London show. I thought it might be a good idea if I had a chat with her first.'

Brel shrugged. His head was hurting, and he didn't bother to correct Terry's assumption about Gerald's source of information. He saw no reason to mention the boy in Kalman's office who — for a fee — had been anxious to answer Gerald's questions, nor to involve June Clairvale. Instead he looked pointedly at his watch. 'Hadn't you better hurry?' he said. 'You're going to be late for lunch.'

The Dales departed in haste and some confusion, and Brel went along to the dining-room. On Saturdays the club provided only a buffet lunch with a choice of hot or cold dishes, and on this particular day it obviously wasn't popular.

Brel picked up a tray and moved along the buffet counter. The day was warm. He himself had no desire for hot food, but another member, an elderly novelist, came in behind him and wanted roast beef. There was no one behind the counter to serve him, so he went over to the bell and kept a firm finger on it. Still no one came.

'Heaven knows what's got into this place,' he said to Brel angrily. He gestured towards the service door. 'Listen. You can hear them all cackling away in there instead of paying us any attention.'

Brel smiled his sympathy and beat a hasty retreat to the

cashier. While she totted up his bill he watched the
novelist protesting violently to an equally angry, red-
faced woman who had appeared and was serving him.
When she had finished, she stormed back into the service
quarters.

'More trouble?' Brel said.

The cashier made a face. 'Not really, but everyone's
naturally a bit fraught at the moment, and to top it all
the kitchen ventilation system's gone on the blink.'

'That's can't be much fun for the staff in this weather.'
Brel took out his wallet. 'It's lucky it's the weekend, and
you're not busy.'

'You tell Mr Jenson that.' The cashier lowered her
voice. 'He's making more fuss than anyone. He hates
anything being wrong in the club, anything at all.'

'That's partly what he's here for,' Brel said mildly.

'Of course, sir,' she agreed. 'I don't blame him one bit.
He does a splendid job. But he certainly likes efficiency.'

Brel laughed. He quickly paid for his meal — he didn't
want to delay the irascible novelist who had come up
behind him — and took his tray to a small table near an
open window.

Wrinkling his nose as the smell of exhaust fumes
drifted in from the street below, Brel began to eat. The
food seemed to improve his headache, and for a moment
he reflected with amusement on the secretary's apparent
anger at the failure of the ventilation system. Then,
against his will, his thoughts returned to Gerald Hinton
and the Dales and his own efforts that morning.

He'd achieved very little, he realized — certainly very
little that would be of immediate and direct use to
Gerald. True, he'd learnt a lot about Terry Dale — and
about Sally-Ann Belmont — and he'd at least established
that there was an alternative candidate for the honour of
fathering her child. But his mind boggled at the Lydneys'
reaction to a vituperative and probably inconclusive

argument between their future son-in-law and Terry Dale over the question of paternity. Blood tests and medical evidence of that sort might help, but if the Belmont girl persisted with her accusation against Gerald, the Lydneys would be almost certain to accept her claims at their face value, especially in view of their inbuilt objections to the marriage of Gerald and Elizabeth.

Brel shook his head. The whole thing was just too damn complicated, and basically none of his business. Then he remembered Peter Dale's crack about Sally-Ann going away for the weekend. He wondered if she really had acquired another boy-friend to replace Terry. Brel ruminated about this possibility for a few minutes, but again it seemed a fairly useless speculation.

'Dr Breland, sir.'

Brel looked up, startled. The young man who had earlier served drinks in the drawing-room was standing in front of him.

'Yes. Yes, what is it?' Brel spoke more sharply than he had intended.

'Beg pardon, sir, but—but—' The barman stuttered.

Brel recollected himself. 'What is it?' he repeated mildly, grinning. 'I'm sorry. I was lost in thought.'

'Sir, it's like this. If you wouldn't mind, Myrtle Cain would like a word with you. She's waiting in the corridor outside the temporary ladies'. The police have still got the proper cloakroom sealed. I'll show you, sir,' he said eagerly.

Brel swallowed the last of his cheese. 'And who's Myrtle Cain?' he asked.

'Myrtle's a friend of Dora's, sir. You know, Dora Brown, the cloakroom lady who got killed.'

'Yes, I know who Mrs Brown is—was,' Brel said slowly. 'And her friend wants to speak to me.'

'That's right, sir. Yes.' The barman nodded vigorously,

as if pleased that Brel had at last grasped the point. 'She's waiting for you.'

Brel pushed back his chair. 'Okay,' he said. 'Lead on.'

CHAPTER 10

Alan Jenson had been ingenious. The police had completed their examination of the club's ladies' cloakroom, but had then sealed the area, thus creating a major crisis. Naturally, staff dressing-rooms and washrooms were available, but the secretary thought these unsuitable and inconvenient for members. Instead, he had commandeered two of the larger bedrooms on the third floor, opened the communicating door between them and rearranged the furniture. With their en suite bathrooms they provided excellent temporary facilities.

This arrangement had one disadvantage, of which only the club servants were aware. The new rooms were considerably more isolated than the regular cloakroom, and Myrtle Cain, the attendant, was unhappy. Mrs Cain was a temporary employee, recommended by Dora Brown some weeks ago to work alternate shifts with her. She was hoping to become part of the regular club staff, and everyone agreed that this was no time for her to raise objections and thus forfeit the secretary's goodwill. It was difficult for them to understand her problem, for she was at least ten years younger than Dora and a bigger, active woman, and no one would have thought of her as nervous or suggestible.

The young barman explained all this to Brel as they went up in the lift. He found the doctor sympathetic, and had almost lost his stutter. 'Mrs Cain said it was very important, sir, else I wouldn't have troubled you. She said she wanted to see you urgently.'

'Do you think she's feeling ill?'

'Oh no. Not at all, Doctor. She's just plain scared.'

Trying to absorb this judgement, Brel followed the barman out of the lift and along a corridor to a door marked by a neatly hand-lettered sign: 'Ladies Cloakroom'. The young man knocked, and at once the door was opened by a woman wearing the club's regulaton black skirt and white blouse.

She stared at them. 'Oh,' she said. 'Thanks very much.' She nodded her dismissal to the barman. She turned to Brel. 'You're Dr Breland. I'm sorry to bother you, sir.'

'That's all right. What can I do for you, Mrs Cain?' Brel consciously spoke a little heartily. She looked to him as if she were normally a calm, self-possessed woman, but he could see the tell-tale signs of nervous tension in the movement of her eyes and in her hands, which were unconsciously washing each other. He smiled at her reassuringly. 'You're not ill?'

'No, no, sir. It's nothing like that. I'm well enough, but I've got to talk to someone and I hoped you—you—'

'Of course, Mrs Cain.' Brel didn't ask why she had chosen him to confide in. As a doctor he wasn't unused to being treated as a substitute priest, and he knew that patients had always seemed to find him particularly easy to talk to. He looked up and down the corridor. At one end, in a window alcove, were two fairly comfortable-looking chairs with a small table between them. He gestured. 'We could sit there, if you can leave your post for a few minutes.'

'Oh yes, please. There are almost no ladies in the club today. The place is practically deserted.'

She spoke clearly and pleasantly, but with an underlying note of eagerness, almost hysteria. Brel glanced at her sharply, and he wasn't surprised when she suddenly gave a convulsive shudder. Then she squared her shoulders and marched along to the alcove. She sat down heavily at once, formality forgotten in the nervous strain of the moment.

'It's about Dora Brown,' she said abruptly.

'She was a friend of yours?' Brel asked encouragingly.

Myrtle Cain nodded. 'We live in the same street. I mean, we did. I was very fond of Dora. She was a nice woman, a good woman. No one could have wanted her dead, certainly not young Doug. He's made himself sick grieving for her.'

She hesitated, and Brel said, 'It seems someone had it in for Dora.'

'No,' said Myrtle Cain. 'No, I don't think so. Dr Breland, I believe she was killed instead of me. That's why—'

'What do you mean—instead of?'

'By mistake for, sir. The murderer meant to kill me, not her. I changed shifts with Dora that evening. It was my wedding anniversary last Thursday and there was a party at home. We're not really supposed to swap shifts without permission, but of course we do it all the time. I think someone believed I was on duty . . . Dr Breland, the police haven't found any reason for Dora's death, have they—I mean, apart from this silly idea about Doug?'

'I've no idea what the police think, but as far as I know they haven't. But why you, Mrs Cain? Who would want to kill you? Have you got enemies, or—'

'That's the point, Doctor. I have. Or I think I might have.' Myrtle Cain's eyes began to water as she looked away from Brel. 'It's my brother. His name's Tom Sullivan. He came out of prison ten days ago, and I haven't seen him—'

'Were you close to each other, or—'

Mrs Cain shook her head in a kind of despair. 'I shopped him, Doctor, and he threatened me. I had to do it. He was on the drugs, the hard stuff. You know, he was stealing to get the cash for it. It wasn't right. And I'm afraid he's dangerous. God knows what he'll do now, but I think—he'll—try—'

As her words became increasingly incoherent, she stopped speaking, and blinked away the tears from her eyes. Brel gave her full marks. He said gently, 'Just supposing you're right, and he did want to get at you, why should he come here?'

She stared at him. 'I don't know, Doctor. But he might not want to do me at home. He could easily find out about the club. Plenty of people on the street know where I work, and when. And if he'd thought I was on duty that night . . . Dora and I aren't much alike, but the uniform would be the same. He'd be in a hurry—high on drugs perhaps, if he'd got hold of something. Oh, Doctor, you can see how it could have happened . . . I feel so bad about Dora . . .'

Brel looked out of the window beside him, pondering. He had never stayed at the club, and the view over what he realized must be the flat roof of the kitchen area, little more than a couple of feet below the level of the window-sill, was new to him. There were some mysterious-looking vertical pipes with cowls, the curved top of a large metal ventilation shaft, a covered tank, a few empty flower-pots, sparrows feeding on crumbs generously thrown from the breakfast tray of an overnight visitor. Totally enclosed, on three sides by the club premises and on the fourth by the back of an office block, it was, on a Saturday afternoon when the club was almost empty and the offices shut, a strangely private place.

Brel's gaze was on this scene, but his mind was on Mrs Cain. He was sorry for the woman and would like to help her if he could, and he could see at once a flaw in her argument. The police had not released any exact details of the murder, and in spite of the rumours undoubtedly circulating in the club, Myrtle Cain was probably unaware that Dora had been knifed from the front, thus precluding any chance of misidentification. Still, as she said, there was the possibility of some drug-induced state, which might have made her brother kill merely because he'd been seen where he shouldn't be. Unlikely, perhaps . . .

Nevertheless, relevant or not, Chief Superintendent Freeman must be told of Myrtle Cain's story. Maybe he could arrange protection for her. At least he could establish Tom Sullivan's whereabouts.

'Why haven't you mentioned this to the police or anyone, Mrs Cain?' he asked.

'Party for my brother's sake, if I'm wrong, and partly because of my job. I'm only a temporary, and no one would want to employ a cloakroom attendant whose brother was a drug addict and a jailbird. You should see the furs we get in here some nights . . . And Mr Jenson's so strict. I'm still hoping it won't all have to come out, but if people saw me going to the police, they'd start to wonder . . .'

'But the police have got to be told, you know. This could make a lot of difference.'

'I know. That's why I wanted to talk to you. Doctor, I was hoping you'd tell them—for me, you know. Then, if they want to, they could see me outside, and if Tom's cleared no one—not Mr Jenson or anyone—need know anything about it. Then I might get Dora's job permanently.' Mrs Cain stopped suddenly. 'Oh, that sounds awful. But you know what I mean. It's a good job, and there's not much money coming into the house at the moment.'

'I understand, Mrs Cain.' Brel suppressed a sigh. He couldn't refuse. He touched the bump where Peter Dale had coshed him, and wondered why he allowed himself to get involved in other people's affairs. 'I'll pass on what you've told me to the Superintendent, and if there's any trouble with Mr Jenson I'll do what I can.'

'Oh, thank you, sir. Thank you very much.'

Brel stood up. Through the window he saw two men in blue boiler suits emerge from a door set in the left-hand wall of the club and walk out across the roof. They made for the ventilation shaft. Fleetingly he thought that Myrtle Cain was much better off in the temporary ladies' cloakroom, however isolated, than in the hot, apparently unventilated kitchens below.

He said, knowing it wasn't a helpful remark, 'Don't worry, Mrs Cain. Everything'll be all right.'

Brel found Chief Superintendent Freeman and Sergeant Anderson in the room they had made their headquarters. Seated on either side of a table, they were busy having lunch. Heaped plates and tankards of beer suggested that they were being well looked after.

'May I interrupt?'

'Sure, Dr Breland,' Freeman said. 'Come along in. Found some more evidence for us?'

'Yes. I think so.'

'Well, fine, as long as we don't have to take any action before we've finished this. We don't often do so splendidly. Usually it's sandwiches in a pub when we're on a case, or tea slopped in a saucer. But your secretary's doing us proud.' Freeman grinned. 'Let's have it.'

Brel pulled up a chair and sat down beside them. While the two officers ate and drank he repeated Myrtle Cain's story as briefly as possible, and very tentatively added his own comments.

'It's really nothing to do with me,' he concluded, 'but I hope you'll see the woman's point and not make trouble for her if you can help it.'

'Sure, sure. We'll take care. We always do. But hell! We should have been told all this yesterday at the latest. What did you say the brother's name was?'

'Tom Sullivan,' put in the sergeant, who had been taking notes.

'Okay. Get on to it, will you, Sergeant. Get his file and have his dabs checked against the ones we found here. If he's just come out of stir, he'll be on parole. Find his parole officer, then find Sullivan and see what he was up to on Thursday night. But be tactful with the sister — Mrs Cain, was it? Interview her outside the club to start with.'

'Right away, sir.' Sergeant Anderson finished his beer, grinned at Brel and made for the door.

'How are things going?' Brel asked, a little hesitantly.

Chief Superintendent Freeman showed no objection to the question. He threw up his hands in mock despair and said, 'Nowhere, fast. The damn case is making no progress at all. And you know why, Doctor. It's because nobody tells us anything.'

'As far as Mrs Cain's concerned, you can see why,' said Brel. 'Her reaction's not unreasonable.'

'Sure,' said the Chief Superintendent again. 'Sure. Anyway, we've now got two runners — young Doug and this guy Sullivan. Doug's a non-starter if ever I saw one, but Sullivan — he could be different. I find it hard to believe he mistook poor little sick Dora for anyone else, but he could have killed her, as you say, just because she saw him. That idea would hold more water if he'd been pinching something — Lady Wander's mink coat, for instance. According to Sir Richard — and he paid for it so he ought to know — it's worth several thousand quid. But nothing was stolen . . .'

'Did you say "sick Dora"?' Brel interrupted, immediately interested. 'What was the trouble? Was she under medical care?'

'Yes. She'd got some kind of high blood pressure. Essential hypertension, the quack —' Freeman looked up at Brel and grinned. 'Sorry, Doctor. Apparently it's what you call high blood pressure when you don't know why

someone's got it. A chronic nuisance, but not likely to kill
you if you take care. But you'd know more about that
than I do.'

'Yes, I understand,' said Brel. 'It's a difficult condition
to treat with any success.'

At that moment there was a sharp knock at the door,
and they both turned quickly as a young uniformed
constable came in, a man in a blue boiler suit at his heels.
Both men looked sickly pale.

'Super, sir — there's a — a young woman in the kitchen
ventilation shaft. Jock here found her.'

'Is there now? Dead?'

'Yes, sir.'

In spite of the studied calmness of his initial question,
the Chief Superintendent's reaction was swift. He was a
big, heavily-built man but he was light on his feet, and he
was half way to the door before Brel had moved. 'Show
me,' he said quietly.

In the absence of any orders to the contrary, Brel
sprinted after them. Up the stairs, two at a time, along a
corridor, through a fire door, a short passage, a couple of
steps and another door, opening on to a flat roof. Brel
knew where he was immediately. It was the scene he'd
watched through the window as he'd talked to Myrtle
Cain. But now his senses were heightened. The sky was a
deeper blue, the lead roofing a deeper grey, the sun
brighter, the windows in the surrounding buildings more
opaque.

Then, as he caught up with the Chief Superintendent,
the second maintenance man, who had been standing
beside the large curved ventilation shaft, shifted his
position. And Brel saw, lying on the ground, a long
bundle rolled up in what appeared to be a dirty blanket.
Two stockinged feet stuck out at one end. My God,
thought Brel, two bodies in three days.

Chief Superintendent Freeman knelt beside the

bundle. 'Have you touched it?' he asked at once.

'We had to get it out of the shaft, hadn't we?' The maintenance man was slightly aggressive. 'We didn't know what it was to start with.'

'Of course, of course. But since then, have you touched it?'

'I had a peep, only enough to see it was a young woman, and dead. Then I sent Jock for your people.'

Freeman knelt and gently unwound the blanket, exposing the blonde hair, the pallid face, the staring blue eyes and the upper part of the body. The golden material of the dress shimmered in the sunlight. The blood on the front of it had long since dried.

'At least we've got a doctor on the spot again,' Freeman said, standing up and making room for Brel. 'Just look. Don't disturb anything. What do you think?'

'Stabbed, I guess,' Brel said after a moment. 'A day or two ago probably, just like . . .'

'Fine. That's enough for now. We'll get our own man here soon,' Freeman interrupted. He added. 'By the looks of her she wasn't a cloakroom attendant.'

'No. She wasn't. She was an actress, a model. Her name was Sally-Ann Belmont,' Brel replied, and he was angry that his voice shook.

The Chief Superintendent looked round sharply. 'Helpful as always, Dr Breland. I don't know what we'd do without you.' His glance was searching. 'Friend of yours?'

'No. Not exactly.'

Brel's mind raced as Freeman issued a series of rapid orders to the constable beside him. The police surgeon, a team from the Yard, the pathologist, an ambulance. Sally-Ann was dead, clearly murdered in the same way and probably on the same night as Dora Brown, the night of Gerald's party. Obviously the murders were connected in some way. But how? And why? What he had to do,

Brel realized, was to get away by himself and think the whole thing through, before Freeman started asking awkward questions. Instinctively he began to move towards the door leading from the roof, but the Chief Superintendent sensed his intention and put a hand on his arm. 'Bear with me till my chaps arrive,' he said. 'Then we'll have a talk.'

The thought of the interview and the inevitable statement, and the questions he might not want to answer, or answer fully, brought a wry twist to Brel's mouth.

CHAPTER 11

The Chief Superintendent wasted no time. Forty-five minutes later, after the police reinforcements had arrived and the routine had been set in motion, Brel found himself once again in the small smoking-room that was serving as Freeman's office. By some feat of official technology Sergeant Anderson had been retrieved from his search for Tom Sullivan and was sitting in his usual chair, notebook open before him. Looking back on the time since he had identified the body, Brel realized that unobtrusively but firmly he had been given no chance to make phone calls or contact anyone in privacy and without the knowledge of the police.

'Well now, Dr Breland. Perhaps you'd be good enough to tell us all you know about this Sally-Ann Belmont.'

The wording was different but it amounted to the same thing, Brel thought, only now he wasn't interrogating the Dales, he himself was being interviewed by the authorities. Personally, he had nothing to hide, and no reason to lie to the police or be less than frank with them. The problem was that Gerald Hinton was obviously in deep trouble, and Gerald was his friend. It was a classic dilemma — his duty as a citizen versus his feelings as an individual. It was hard to decide how far he should cooperate with the Chief Superintendent. His attitude was coloured by the fact that Freeman's attitude to himself since the scene on the kitchen roof seemed to have subtly shifted. No longer were they quasi-professional colleagues; in some curious way they had become antagonists. And this Brel resented. He felt as if, through no fault of his own, he had been firmly marked as an adversary of the police.

He said, 'I met Miss Belmont for the first time last Tuesday.' He stopped, for he had surprised himself by his own statement. It was difficult to believe that five days ago he had never heard of the girl. With an effort, wondering if his involuntary pause had aroused Freeman's suspicions in some way, he went on. 'She came to me as a patient. As I said, it was the first time I'd seen her. She said she was four months pregnant and complained of abdominal pain. I examined her in the presence of my nurse, and — '

'What's your nurse's name, Doctor?' said Sergeant Anderson, pencil poised.

Brel looked at him in surprise. 'Mrs Kathleen Taylor,' he replied. 'She'll confirm all this, I assure you, if that's what you're after.'

'Now, Doctor, don't get annoyed.' Freeman intervened. 'It's just routine. Sergeant Anderson knows I'd get mad later if we hadn't got all the details.'

Brel said, 'All right. I understand. Well, I examined her in the presence of my nurse, but I could find nothing wrong. However, in view of her pregnancy, I advised her to see a consultant gynaecologist. All my notes are in my Harley Street rooms, Chief Superintendent.'

'Harley Street, yes. Weren't you a little surprised to see her, Doctor? Your practice isn't the kind where people just turn up at surgery hours, is it?'

It was a question Brel had expected. 'No, not normally. Miss Belmont told my secretary—Mrs Taylor's also my secretary, Sergeant, though she's a qualified nurse—she told my secretary she was a friend of Gerald Hinton, who's also a friend of mine. Incidentally, we were able to fit Miss Belmont in at short notice because we'd had an unexpected cancellation.'

'So Mr Hinton could probably tell us more about Miss Belmont,' said Freeman reasonably.

'No, that's the point,' said Brel. 'Gerald denies knowing her at all. I asked him specially because I discovered that Miss Belmont had lied to me. The name and address she gave me for her own general practitioner were quite false—there's no doctor with that name on the Register. And the address she gave as her own—in Cornwall, it was—also seems to be false.'

'What made you check all this, Dr Breland? Did something strike you as odd?' asked Freeman.

'No, not at first. I merely wanted to confirm her GP's name to write him a note. Then, when I found he was a phoney, I naturally made enquiries. It was odd, as you say, but I didn't bother all that much because I never expected to see her again—and she'd paid her bill before she left,' Brel added with an attempt at humour. He was rewarded by a slight smile from the Chief Superintendent. 'However . . .' he went on.

Brel told the story of Gerald Hinton's stag party, and Sally-Ann Belmont's dramatic intervention absolutely straight. He commented that what had at first had the appearance of a joke had soon turned into a seemingly vicious attack, and he admitted that Gerald had been very upset. He said nothing about the reactions of his fellow-guests; they could speak for themselves, he thought.

When he finished Chief Superintendent Freeman sat

back in his chair and stared out of the window. Then he reached for a file. 'In his statement about Dora Brown Mr Hinton said that he caught sight of a friend who disappeared into the ladies' cloakroom. That would have been Miss Belmont?'

'Yes, I expect so,' said Brel. Really, he thought, this was impossible. It was essential that he should get together with Gerald and compare their stories. Then he thought, stories! Why should we be telling 'stories'? We've got nothing to hide. Or do I believe that Gerald did have a hand in two murders?

'So while he was waiting for her to come out he'd have had ample opportunity to take the dagger from the display case.' It seemed to Brel that the Chief Superintendent's manner had again changed. Once more he was treating Brel more as a colleague than a suspect. Maybe it was nothing but an interviewing trick, but he couldn't prevent himself from responding.

'Sure! Then he persuaded Sally-Ann to go up to his room, killed her, stuffed her down the ventilation shaft, went back to the ladies' and killed Dora Brown, and returned to the party as if nothing had happened?'

The Chief Superintendent ignored the mild sarcasm. 'It needn't have been quite like that,' he replied. 'And you said yourself, Doctor, that Mr Hinton was upset when he went after Miss Belmont. Now, what about the timing? How long was he away from the party?'

'How should I know?'

'You were there.'

'I was there all right. But we'd all had a good deal to drink, Chief Superintendent. People took the chance to go and pee. Some of them were away ages. Terry Dale never came back. He was sick. His brother took him up to their room. As far as Gerald was concerned, I'd say ten, fifteen, twenty minutes. You'll have to ask him.'

'Oh, I shall, Doctor. Everyone at the party will be

questioned, I assure you. Fourteen of you altogether, you said? Let's make sure we've got their names right. You can help us check them against this list of people who were in the club that night.'

Brel nodded. He was reminded that Gerald, now at the Lydneys', was happily unaware of how his troubles had mushroomed. God! He must do his best to warn him before the police turned up on the doorstep.

Brel said, 'It was Hinton's party, not mine, you know, Chief Superintendent, but I can tell you the names of almost all the people who were there. Jenson, the club secretary, probably has a complete guest list.'

'Fair enough. In the meantime, let's go through the ones you do know.'

Brel mentioned Jack Dawson, Charles Lydney, Nick Ryle, the Dale brothers and most of the others, adding odd items of information and relationship about each of them.

'That's been most helpful. Thank you, Doctor.'

Brel realized that Freeman's attitude had encouraged him to be candid, but he was worried about the implications of what he'd said for Gerald. 'Not at all,' he replied. 'But before you start jumping to conclusions—'

'I never jump to conclusions, Doctor.'

'No, I don't think you do,' said Brel slowly, smiling. 'What I meant was, before you make any tentative judgements, you should know that Gerald Hinton spent the best part of yesterday trying to track down Sally-Ann Belmont. He had to find her to get her to recant what she'd said about her child on Thursday night. I was with him most of the time, and I can tell you now that his actions weren't those of someone who knew she was already dead.'

Again Brel launched into an explanation. At least this was in Gerald's favour, he thought. But the Chief Superintendent, though he listened carefully, showed no reaction, and Brel could not guess what he was thinking.

'Mr Hinton's a keen theatre-goer?' It was more a statement than a question.

'Yes, when he's in London,' Brel agreed. 'As you'd expect, a lot of members of the Arts and Letters are. Some of them are closely connected with it. For instance, someone told me that Sir Richard Wander's one of the angels of *Sirens on the Wind*.'

'You mean he's backing it — put some money into the show.'

'Yes. I've no idea how much. It's not unusual, you know, especially these days. Many shows are backed by syndicates of interested people.'

Chief Superintendent Freeman grunted. 'So he might know Miss Belmont?'

'Not necessarily, but he might, yes. Terry Dale knew her; she worked for him in some TV commercial once.' Brel stopped, wondering why he was volunteering this information. He had no great liking for the Dales at the moment, and Terry had certainly had both motive and opportunity to get rid of the Belmont girl, but that was no reason to go out of his way to throw suspicion on him. 'He could probably help you more than I can,' Brel concluded weakly.

'You've been a great help, Doctor.' Freeman suddenly beamed. 'Don't think you haven't. Now, got all your notes, Sergeant? Good. If there's nothing else, we must —'

But there was something else, Brel thought, and he hesitated whether to mention it — Sally-Ann Belmont's evening bag now sitting on the table in the hall of her flat. Probably by now one of the Chief Superintendent's minions had already discovered — from Roberts or one of the maids — where it had been found. In any case, it was only a matter of time before Freeman knew. Yesterday it had seemed just another ridiculous and unnecessarily vicious part of the hoax. Today it had become a damning piece of evidence against Gerald — possibly more damning if it was left unmentioned now. But mentioning it would involve complicated explanations of his own somewhat ambiguous behaviour — and the Dales'. Brel was shaking his head in doubt, when a tap at the door was followed by the entry of the police surgeon.

' 'Afternoon,' Dr Forsyth said. He yawned and grinned at Brel. 'If you've got to have another murder in your club, why choose a Saturday? It's not the sort of thing a man welcomes after a morning of golf and a large lunch.'

'Saturday? You don't mean she was killed today, this morning?' Freeman picked up the point quickly.

'No, no. Just a manner of speaking.' The police surgeon sat himself down and stretched his legs out in front of him. 'Time of death, between twenty-four and forty-eight hours ago, but don't hold me to it. Cause of death, stab through the heart, with a downwards blow from right to left, I think. Whoever did it was probably taller than she was — and she was quite a big girl — or she was sitting down and not expecting it. And, if you want another guess before the body's been examined properly, the weapon was our old friend Hamlet's dagger. I lay odds they'll find her blood corresponds with the second lot forensic came up with on the handle — the sample that wasn't Dora Brown's.'

'Thanks.' The Chief Superintendent nodded his appreciation. 'You've been very quick.'

'Any time,' said Forsyth. He held up an admonishing hand. 'But it's only preliminary, you know. They're taking the body away for the PM now. You should have the results in the morning at the latest.'

'Sure, I know,' said Freeman. 'But your guesses usually turn out right.'

Brel said tentatively, 'I didn't realize there were two blood groups on the dagger.'

'Oh, I thought I'd mentioned it to you.' Freeman

looked at Brel as if challenging him to question this
remark. 'Well, we'll soon know more about it. You'll be
around tomorrow, Dr Breland?'

'Tomorrow's Sunday.'

'Yes. We work on Sundays sometimes. But you won't
be?'

'No. One of my partners is covering for me this
weekend. But I wasn't planning to come down to the
club.'

'We could get you at home if necessary?'

'Of course. I imagine I'll have to sign another
statement.'

'I'm afraid so, Doctor. Sergeant Anderson's going to
draft it now. Routine, you know. Sorry to bother you
after all your help.'

'That's all right.'

The interview was clearly over. Without showing too
much eagerness, Brel said his goodbyes and made his
escape, secretly blessing the police surgeon. Forsyth's
timely arrival had saved him from an awkward dilemma.
When he was questioned later he could always plead that
he had been about to tell Freeman about Sally-Ann's
evening bag when Forsyth interrupted, and in course of
the following conversation it had slipped his mind. Or as
a last resort he could always fall back on a reasonable
reluctance to cast suspicion on a friend.

Anyway he had bought time to think and plan
and—most important of all—contact Gerald. Warning
Gerald was the first priority, and for that he needed a
phone. The club's telephones were a little public. The
best and simplest thing was to go home to the flat.

It wasn't as easy to warn Gerald as Brel had expected. In
fact, even getting in touch with him presented
unexpected difficulties. Brel knew the name of the village
on the Kent-East Sussex border near the Lydneys' house,

so he dialled directory enquiries and, after the usual interminable delay, a voice answered. Eventually, he was informed, slightly acidly, that the name Lydney did not appear in either of the relevant books.

'Archibald Lydney must be there.' Impatiently Brel spelt the name again.

There was yet another lengthy pause. Brel caught himself drumming on the telephone table.

'I'm sorry, but there's no Lydney listed in that area. Of course, it may be an unlisted number.'

'Can you tell me if it is? Please . . .'

'It wouldn't do you any good. I'm not allowed to give it out.' The voice spoke as if to a child. 'The whole point of numbers being unlisted is that people can't telephone them.'

Brel banged down the receiver, and racked his brains trying to think who might know the Lydneys' number. Charles was spending the weekend with his parents, and Nick Ryle had gone with him. Who else was there? The Dawsons, perhaps.

He tried their number and explained his problem to Jack Dawson. 'Do you know the number?' he asked.

'No. It's just possible Marjorie might, but I doubt it. Hang on.'

Brel hung on. If Marjorie couldn't help there would be nothing for it but a drive down to the Lydneys, he decided. He hadn't got the exact address, but in a small village surely the publican or someone would know where the Lydneys lived.

'Brel.' Jack had returned to the phone. 'No luck. I'm sorry, Marjorie hasn't the faintest idea. She's never had any reason to call them. Is it important?'

'Very.' Brel didn't hesitate. Gerald was going to need all the friends he had, and the Dawsons were very close to him. 'Jack, have you told Marjorie what happened at Gerald's party?'

'Yes. She was shocked about that woman's death, of
course. But she hooted with laughter about the gorgeous
blonde. She swears Gerald's so besotted with Elizabeth
that even Helen of Troy wouldn't get a second glance
from him, and—'

'Jack!' Brel's sharp interruption cut off Dawson's
amused flow of words.

'Yes? What is it, Brel?'

'Marjorie may have to swear to something like that for
real—in court. The gorgeous blonde's been found dead,
murdered, at the club. It's not going to be pleasant for
Gerald.'

'Christ! But why—'

Briefly Brel told Jack Dawson what had happened, and
how he had become involved. He ended by saying, 'I'll
leave it to you what you tell Marjorie, but when the police
get in touch with you—and they will—you'd better not
mention this conversation. Okay?'

'Sure, if you'll get hold of Gerald.'

Reflecting grimly that he was now, at least
involuntarily, in the business of obstructing the police in
the course of their enquiries, Brel hesitated before getting
in touch with the Dales, and almost instantly decided
against it. They would still be enjoying—or suffering—
Jennifer's lunch-party, and he wasn't going to annoy her
again. Besides, he saw no reason to compromise himself
further for the sake of Terry Dale and his brother—
certainly not until he had the whole situation much
clearer in his mind. It was Gerald he must speak to before
anyone else.

And, more importantly, he must think—think—of his
own position. In his profession, he was very vulnerable,
and though Freeman might have seemed to become more
friendly, there was no knowing what was really in his
mind.

★

Ten minutes later, Brel hurried from the house and ran to his car. The Lydneys lived in a village called Blackfield, half way between Tunbridge Wells and East Grinstead. He decided that the Sevenoaks-Tonbridge road would be the best approach. Fortunately at this time on a Saturday afternoon there would be very little traffic leaving London, and once he was free of the centre of the city, he could probably make quite good time.

As he started the car and set off towards the river, it was the hoaxer that came first to mind, because it was clearly the hoaxer who had introduced Sally-Ann Belmont into the Arts and Letters Club. Brel was surprised how much he seemed to know about the man.

The hoaxer must have had at least a remote acquaintance with Sally-Ann Belmont, for he'd been able to persuade or bribe her into playing her part. And he'd briefed her very well and accurately, which meant that he knew a good deal about Gerald Hinton. He'd known, for instance, that Gerald was giving a stag party at the Arts and Letters before his wedding at the end of the month, and he'd known the date and exact timing of the party. He'd also known that a Harley Street physician called John Breland was a friend of Gerald's, and would be a guest at the party.

But the most obvious motive was to put an end to Gerald's wedding plans, and for this the prime candidate was, and always had been, Nick Ryle, in spite of his denials, and possibly with Charles Lydney's connivance. For example, there was the fact that Sally-Ann, in the course of her tirade, had referred to 'Liz—or whatever she calls herself'. This might have been chance—she'd shortened Gerald's name too and no one had ever called him 'Gerry'—but it could be significant that only Nick and Charles normally called Elizabeth by the diminutive.

There was, however, one great objection to Ryle as a suspect. Though Ryle might not have expected Gerald to trace Sally-Ann Belmont with such relative ease and speed, he must have assumed that she would be found sooner or later. Once found, there was no guarantee she would persist with her accusation. In fact, faced with threats of legal action, she would have been much more likely to cave in and give Ryle away. And what would Elizabeth think of Cousin Nick then? Maybe the argument was a little convoluted, but Ryle was quite smart enough to appreciate the possibilities.

Held up by traffic lights on his way through south-west London, Brel frowned fiercely about him. He realized he'd just established a perfectly good murder motive for a man he scarcely knew. If the hoax was intended to stick, Sally-Ann had to be permanently removed, and if suspicion could be thrown on Gerald in the process, so much the better.

Brel swore aloud. Surely he was wrong about Nick Ryle. The hoax—yes, perhaps, he might have planned that immature piece of sadism in the hope of preventing Gerald's marriage to Elizabeth. But it was hard to believe that Ryle had thought through the rest of it—to the ultimate, almost inevitable, end of premeditated murder. Besides, he wasn't a member of the Arts and Letters Club and wouldn't be familiar with its layout. Further, Charles Lydney had left the party in the dining-room and returned with him, and Lydney certainly wasn't such a fool as to get involved in murder merely for the sake of avoiding an undesirable brother-in-law.

Brel continued to ruminate. Assume that the hoaxer and the killer were not one and the same—what then? In that case, Sally-Ann's murder was presumably unpremeditated; it could be said to bear the signs of something hurried and ill-conceived. This was the case against Gerald. If he had persuaded Sally-Ann to go up to his room, if he'd tried to bribe her to admit to her masquerade and she'd mocked him and refused, if he'd already taken the dagger as a possible threat, if Dora Brown had seen him replacing the dagger . . . If . . . If . . .

Brel shook his head angrily, and immediately regretted it as a dull pain throbbed behind his eyes. His headache, eased by the whisky before lunch and the food, was beginning to return. It reminded him forcibly that Gerald and Nick Ryle weren't the only people with possible motives for wishing Sally-Ann dead.

He had good reason to know that Peter Dale was a violent man, and prepared to defend his brother's interests. The Dales had both been staying at the club that night; in fact, Terry Dale had never returned to the party. They were big men and it would have been easy for them to push Sally-Ann out of the window and thrust her into the ventilation shaft. The two of them together could have done the job much more easily than Gerald by himself. Using the dagger from the display case could be taken to indicate either careful planning or hasty improvisation. And Dora Brown? Presumably she'd seen something. And what about Sally-Ann's bag, found under Gerald's bed? A hasty addition to the hoax, or a planted red herring? Brel sighed. All this analysis was getting nowhere; its only result had been to make his headache worse.

Angry at his inability to draw any reasonable conclusions from the evidence, Brel put his foot down hard on the accelerator. He was nearly into Tunbridge Wells, and only fifteen minutes or so from the Lydneys' village. The need to talk to Gerald was still paramount.

CHAPTER 12

It was almost six o'clock when Brel reached Blackfield. He was hot, tired and disgruntled, and his head throbbed gently. He had lost his way after leaving the main road at Tunbridge Wells, and had been forced to make what seemed a very long detour. What a waste of a perfect summer's day! But still, he and Gerald Hinton had been good friends for a long time, and he'd have thought less of himself if he'd deserted Gerald now.

Blackfield turned out to be a most attractive place, still largely unspoilt, with a triangular village green dominated by the Black Swan. The publican was inspecting his window-boxes.

Brel drew up beside him. 'Excuse me,' he said. 'I'm looking for Holmwood House. Do you know it?'

'Sure.' The man came to the side of the car. 'Along there. Second on the left. First on the left. Second on the right. It's just about a mile from here. Big house with a large garden. You can't miss it. The name's on the gatepost at the end of the drive.'

Brel had to ring three times before the front door was eventually opened by Elizabeth Lydney. Fair hair a little rumpled, as if she'd just run her fingers through it, face slightly flushed, she stood and stared at him.

'Hello, Elizabeth. Do you remember me? John Breland. Dr Breland. Gerald's friend. We met at the Dawsons.'

Her expression became more welcoming. 'Oh, hello,' she said. 'This is a surprise.'

'Elizabeth! Who is it?'

A middle-aged woman had come into the hall. Her resemblance to Elizabeth was such that Brel had no doubt who she was. Isobel? Isobel Lydney? Yes, he was sure

Gerald had mentioned the name. She was a shorter, older but still pretty version of her daughter. Brel turned to her.

'Mrs Lydney, I'm John Breland. I know your son and I'm a friend of Gerald Hinton. I need to speak to him. May I come in, please?'

'Yes. Yes, of course.' Mrs Lydney gave him a polite smile. 'I'm afraid we're a little disorganized. It's a slight — er — family crisis.'

Brel nodded. The remark was clearly one of the understatements of the year. From a room on the right, the door of which Mrs Lydney had incautiously left open, the sound of raised, angry voices could be heard. The family and Gerald — Brel recognized his voice — were undoubtedly having an almighty row. And there was no need to make any guesses at the reason for it.

'Despicable! That's the only word for such behaviour. Despicable! Why didn't you tell me about this immediately, Charles?'

'Dad, Gerald said it wasn't true. He thought it was a hoax or a joke of some kind.'

'A hoax? Now, look here, when your sister's involved —'

'Charles and I —'

'To think he should —'

'For God's sake, why can't you listen?'

This last was Gerald's contribution, and was almost a shout. It won Brel's instant sympathy. But it had little effect on Archibald Lydney. His voice continued to override the others.

Mrs Lydney, who had also been listening to this furious dialogue, pulled herself together and turned to Brel. 'Dr Breland, would you come this way, please. If you'll just wait in the study, I'll —'

'No, thank you.' Brel had made up his mind. He would have preferred to confer with Gerald privately, but the time for such niceties seemed to be past. 'I think I'd better go in there and talk to everyone.'

'Oh no—' began Mrs Lydney. Then she caught Brel's determined eye and accepted the inevitable. 'Very well, if you insist. Come along.'

She led the way across the hall to the open door, Elizabeth following them. Beyond the door was a large, elegant room. Brel looked round quickly and took in the huge Chinese carpet, the sofas and armchairs covered in a heavy silk, the antique pieces. The whole thing looked a little too good to be true, too tidy, almost like a stage setting for a drawing-room comedy—or drama. The effect of a set was accentuated by the wide French windows giving on to an immaculate lawn. Nick Ryle was lounging in an armchair in front of them.

The rest of the cast—Gerald, Charles Lydney and a tall, upright man with a beaked nose, greying hair, shaggy eyebrows and glittering blue eyes—were standing in an angry triangle in the middle of the floor. They seemed struck dumb by Brel's sudden entrance, and only Gerald looked remotely pleased to see him.

Mrs Lydney made an ineffectual gesture towards introductions. To her husband, she said, 'Dear, this is—'

Mr Lydney had no time for such formalities. 'Who are you?' he demanded bluntly. 'And what do you want?'

'Dad, this is Brel—Dr Breland—you've heard me speak of him.' At home in the presence of his overbearing father, Charles Lydney had lost a lot of his normal arrogance. 'He was at Gerald's party.'

'Was he indeed?' Archibald Lydney regarded Brel as if he was some particularly lowly member of his workforce. 'Does that give him any right to interrupt a family discussion?'

'You saw her?' Gerald burst in, red-faced with anger. 'You saw her today. You've got her story—her denial? Why didn't you phone?'

Brel shook his head, trying to warn Gerald to keep quiet. 'I'm sorry to arrive like this, sir,' he said soothingly to Mr Lydney, 'but I've got some news—important, but not very good, I'm afraid.' To Gerald, he added, 'You didn't give me the number and it's unlisted. I had to come down myself.'

'What do you mean—not very good?' exclaimed Gerald. 'She won't deny it? But she must! What did she say?'

'Gerald—'

But Mr Lydney wasn't prepared to be ignored any longer. 'What difference does it make if the woman denies anything now? She's made a public accusation, and that's what people'll remember. That's what they'll be saying behind Elizabeth's back.'

'Nonsense!' Gerald shouted. 'There were only fourteen of us there. My friends—most of them.' He glared at Nick Ryle.

'And you think no one'll talk?' Ryle responded immediately. 'I bet it's all over your club already.'

Gerald turned to Brel. 'What the hell did she say?' he demanded. 'Whatever Lydney may think, I want it denied, and I want to know who put her up to it.'

Archibald Lydney opened his mouth to intervene, but Brel forestalled him.

'Sally-Ann Belmont is dead,' he said quietly. 'She was found today, at the club. She'd been killed, stabbed to death, probably on Thursday night.'

For a moment the silence was total. Then there was a babble of voices, asking questions and not waiting for answers, expressing horror but no pity. Only Gerald gave a thought to the murdered girl.

'Poor bitch!' he said. 'Poor bitch.'

Gerald's remark seemed to galvanize Mr Lydney. 'That settles it,' he said. He had moved to the fireplace and he banged his fist down on the mantelshelf to emphasize his words. A Chelsea figurine bounced in the air and was saved from instant disintegration on the hearth by a quick grab from Charles. Brel had to make a conscious effort to restrain himself from nervous laughter. The drama of the situation was rapidly being overlaid by farce.

'That settles it,' Lydney repeated. 'Elizabeth, you must admit this marriage is impossible. You know I've had my doubts all along, and they've been reinforced by this disgraceful story of Gerald and this girl. Now — murder!' He paused, presumably for effect. 'Elizabeth cannot possibly marry this man.'

'And why the hell not?' Gerald said quite calmly. 'Are you accusing me of —'

'There's no need to swear. As for why not, surely it's obvious. You should have cleared up your affairs before you got engaged, before they led to murder!'

'Shit!' Gerald expressed his feelings emphatically, but now without heat. He walked slowly to the door, to stand beside Elizabeth, who had been watching the scene in silence. Her expression was, if anything, judicious, and revealed nothing of her feelings.

'Elizabeth,' Gerald said, 'you can see there's no arguing with your father, or your family. But it's you that matters. You know I love you. I'll always love you. And I want to marry you. I swear to you there's no truth in these — these dreadful stories, these accusations. Will you trust me? I'm going now, but if you can't decide now, don't worry. Take your time. Think about it. I'll be waiting.'

Elizabeth looked at him for a long moment. At last, 'I don't know,' she said. 'I must think.' Suddenly she stood up on tiptoe, took Gerald by his upper arms and kissed him gently on the cheek. Then she ran from the room, and they could all hear the sound of her footsteps on the stairs. After a minute Mrs Lydney followed her.

Gerald turned to Brel. 'Give me five minutes, he said quietly. 'We'll go back to town in convoy.' He left the room without a further word, or a glance at the two Lydney men and Ryle.

Mr Lydney nodded in approval and addressed himself to his son. 'It'll be for the best, Charles,' he said. 'You'll see. Really for the best. Elizabeth's had a lucky escape.'

Aghast at the insensitivity of these remarks, Brel made for the door. 'I'll wait in my car. Goodbye.'

'Good day to you, Doctor. We're grateful to you for clarifying the situation.'

Brel could think of no suitable response to this, Mr Lydney's final comment. Charles followed Brel to the front door, and said, 'We'll see that an announcement's put in the papers, and we'll cope with returning the presents—and the ring. It's all one hell of a nuisance.'

This slightly patronizing remark was the last straw. Brel swung round on Charles. 'It's not your damned decision. It's Elizabeth's. But if anyone's going to have a lucky escape, it's Gerald: he's been saved from marrying into your family. And you can tell your father I said so.'

Brel got into his car and slammed the door without giving Charles a chance to reply. He sat, staring straight ahead of him, waiting for his anger to subside. Minutes later Gerald came out of the house alone, threw his bag into the back of his own car and waved to Brel. They set off, Brel leading.

Just outside Sevenoaks they came to what looked like a pleasant country hotel. There were several cars in the parking lot, so the place was clearly open. There would be drinks, perhaps food. Thinking that they could do with both, Brel signalled to Gerald and drove in.

They were in luck. The barman was happy to give them double whiskies and make suggestions for dinner. Taking the drinks and the menu, Brel led the way into a charming garden that smelt of roses and old-fashioned stock. A few groups were already enjoying the summer evening, but Brel chose a table somewhat apart from the rest, where he and Gerald could talk without being overheard.

As soon as they sat down, Gerald said, 'Brel, you think I did the right thing, don't you? I couldn't press Elizabeth, not just now. I love her. I know we'd be right together. But she's got to decide.'

'Elizabeth seems terrific,' Brel said. 'But her family—whew! Candidly, back there I thought you'd be well out of it, and I damn well told Charles Lydney so. But it's your life, and if you want Elizabeth and she wants you, good luck to you both.'

Brel's mind was on more immediate matters. He knew they must have a serious discussion. He had to awaken Gerald to the full implications of his situation, and make him realize the potential danger of his position.

'About the murders,' he began tentatively, when Gerald surprised him. 'I suppose I'm the main suspect,' he said. 'But I didn't kill the Belmont girl—or the other woman. I'm totally innocent, Brel.'

'I believe you.'

'Thanks.' Gerald smiled, a little wryly. 'But what about the Chief Superintendent—Freeman, was that his name? Does he share your touching faith?'

'I don't know, Gerald. He assures me he never jumps to conclusions, but I don't know.' Brel took a gulp of whisky and waited for the warmth to hit his stomach before he continued. 'There's no getting away from the fact that things look pretty bad for you, at least on the surface. It seems to me that someone's been deliberately setting you up—framing you, if you like—for a manslaughter charge, if not for murder.'

'But who, Brel? I know it must seem like that, but who's going to gain anything from it? Nick Ryle, sure.' Gerald was sad, rather than bitter. 'If Elizabeth decides against me, I suppose he'll marry her. But he'd have to be mad to kill, just to break our engagement. I can't believe that. It's just not on.'

'All right, I agree with you about Nick. Not him. What about the Dales?'

'The Dales? Why?'

Interrupted only by the waiter taking their order for dinner, Brel told Gerald what had happened that morning, and what he'd surmised from it. Long before he'd finished Gerald was shaking his head.

'No, Brel, no. In theory it's possible, I guess. Certainly they could have killed Sally-Ann Belmont perhaps just by accident; they'd hardly have planned a murder at such an obvious time and place. They could have got into my room through the window — I always leave it open — and planted her bag under the bed. But it's absurd. We've been friends for years. They'd never deliberately plan to incriminate me.'

'You were an obvious candidate, Gerald. After the party, no one could say you hadn't got a motive.'

'But I'd have been equally silly to do anything there and then.'

'I know, I know,' said Brel a little irritably. 'Have you got any suggestions — people we haven't thought of? Your business associates, for instance?'

'Business? Oh, come on, Brel. Printing's not like that. Look, I'd take my oath no one, but no one dislikes me — hates me — enough to do this.'

'What about family then?' Brel persisted. 'I heard a story about your father — '

Gerald laughed. 'Oh, that. I'll tell you,' he said.

As soon as the waiter had served their food, he went on. 'It was like this, Brel. There's no real secret about it. My father died last year. Well, when I was going through his papers — I was his executor — I found some letters which made it clear that years ago he'd had an illegitimate child. Apparently he'd been seeing a woman for a long time—it was a kind of stable relationship, if you see what I mean. I must say, in some ways he went up in my estimation. He didn't always have a very happy time at home, you know, in spite of the façade he put up.'

Gerald paused, thinking, then shook his head. 'Anyway the child was a boy—about my own age. I did try to trace him, and his mother. From the letters, my father seems to have promised to take care of them financially, but he certainly didn't mention them in his will.'

Brel was interested. 'You didn't find either of them?'

'No. We'd almost nothing to go on. There was no address on any of the letters she'd written to him, and no second name. I even got my solicitors to advertise in the papers.'

'Were there any answers at all?'

'Oh yes. Over a period. I gather there always are in these circumstances. There were at least a dozen—most of them obvious crooks or cranks—I gather one chap walked out as soon as he discovered there was no question of an immediate inheritance. A couple of others looked likely starters for a while, till the lawyers went into details.'

'What were you going to do if you found them, Gerald?'

'I don't quite know. Make sure they weren't in need or anything, I suppose. I felt a certain affection for the woman—and for my half-brother. Wouldn't you?'

'I imagine so,' said Brel. 'And now? What's the position now?'

'Oh, it's all water under the bridge. I've abandoned the idea. My solicitors were against the whole thing in the first place. They thought it would complicate matters and they wouldn't consider an enquiry agent or anything of that kind. I suppose they had a point; there was no legal claim on the estate.' Gerald grinned. 'Anyway, it'll all be a problem for my own executors. I did insist on that.'

'How do you mean?'

'Well, naturally I had to make a new will right away. I've got no close relatives — no relatives at all that I've seen for many years — so I was going to leave everything to charity. Then it occured to me: it should go to my half-brother, if anyone can ever find him. So I put the necessary instructions in my will. They're to have another go at tracking him down. If they don't succeed in a given time, the charities benefit. As I said, we're much the same age, so it's probably only an outside chance he'll get anything, but you never know. Anyway, it may have been an absurd gesture, but what the hell!' Gerald stopped abruptly and drained his coffee cup. 'I've been talking too much.'

'That's because I've been asking too many questions,' Brel said, 'but I expect the police will do the same. And the sooner the better, I think.' He signalled for their bill. 'We'd better push on Gerald. It'll take us a while to get back to London. We'll phone the Chief Superintendent from Harley Street. With any luck he and his sergeant'll come along and see you there, instead of at the club.'

'Or at Scotland Yard,' said Gerald gloomily.

'You'd better stay the night with me.'

'I'd like that, Brel. I don't think I could bear the club, not today. That's if the police don't cart me away, of course.'

On such a Saturday evening traffic returning to London was heavy, and it was late when they reached Harley Street. The telephone was ringing as they opened the front door of the flat. Guessing it was the Chief Superintendent, Brel swore. He had hoped that Gerald might gain some slight advantage by getting in touch with Freeman first.

'Dr Breland?'

Brel frowned. He didn't recognize the voice. It wasn't

Freeman's and it sounded a little too authoritative for any of Freeman's minions. He couldn't think of a patient who would call his private number, and the tape-machine downstairs would refer any professional calls to Farre.

'Yes, speaking,' he said cautiously.

'Ah, at last. Richard Wander here. I've been trying to get you ever since Jenson rang up with news of this—this fresh disaster at the club. Damnable, absolutely damnable. It'll be splashed across all the Sundays tomorrow. Horrible publicity, not at all what we want.'

'No.' Brel spoke because Sir Richard had stopped, and some response seemed to be expected.

'I want to talk to you about it, Breland. I suppose you couldn't come round now?' Suddenly Sir Richard had become quite diffident.

'I'm afraid not.' Brel was firm. 'It's quite impossible.'

'What about tomorrow morning then? Drinks before lunch?'

'Well—'

'Say twelve-thirty. At my house then. Goodbye.'

The line went dead suddenly, and Brel imagined the receiver being hurriedly replaced as someone entered the room and interrupted Sir Richard, someone he'd not wanted to overhear the call. He'd not even taken the time to give his address. Brel laughed. He scarcely knew Wander; he'd only spoken to him casually half a dozen times at the club. Somehow the unexpected invitation seemed a fitting end to a day of unpleasant surprises.

CHAPTER 13

Brel woke early. In spite of everything it had not been a late night. They had been unable to get in touch with Chief Superintendent Freeman, though they had left urgent messages for him at the club and at New Scotland Yard. Gerald, having talked himself dry over dinner, had been happy to go to bed almost immediately, and Brel had followed soon after.

Now for a full minute he just lay and tried to relax. His bed faced the window and, with the curtains drawn back to let in some air, he could see that it was another beautiful morning. Then he thought of Gerald, and realized resignedly that the night had changed nothing, and that a lovely summer Sunday was about to be devoted to the Belmont affair. Carefully he pushed himself up on the pillows and felt the place behind his ear where Peter Dale had slugged him. It was very tender, but he had no sign of a headache, which was a blessing.

He slid out of bed and went into the bathroom. No headache, no noticeable motor dysfunction, pupils normal, pulse normal, everything normal. Brel grinned at himself in the mirror. In spite of disobeying all the instructions he would have given to a patient after a cranial blow, he was obviously in excellent shape. There was still time for symptoms of concussion to develop, of course, but he had a sense of physical well-being that seemed to deny the possibility.

He went into the kitchen and put on some coffee. By the time it was ready he was showered, shaved and dressed. Passing the door of his minute spare room he was glad to hear a gentle snoring. Gerald had clearly been able to make himself comfortable on the couch there. Good, he thought professionally, a good rest was just what Gerald needed. He drank the coffee and wrote a note — 'Gone for papers. Back for breakfast. Brel.' — which he propped up against the coffee pot. Then he quietly let himself out of the flat.

There were special reasons for getting the Sunday papers today, of course, but it was a ritual that Brel enjoyed at weekends when he was not on call. He walked quickly, his mind on Gerald and the murders. Somehow he felt that the explanation was quite simple, if only he could separate the wood from the trees. The trouble, he thought wryly, was that there were so many damn trees. Maybe the press reports would help to clear his thoughts.

One glance at the piles of newsprint showed him, to his dismay, that the publicity was fierce. Dora Brown's death had made the front pages in yesterday's editions, but today the papers had really gone to town. The story was a natural for the tabloids, of course. SECOND DEATH IN WEST END CLUB — BLONDE MODEL SLAIN was too good a headline for any sub-editor to pass up, and most of them had settled for some variant of this theme.

Unfortunately for the people involved, and for the Arts and Letters Club itself, there was a dearth of serious national or international news this weekend, so that the 'heavies' had led with the murders too. There were pictures of Sally-Ann Belmont on many of the front pages, mostly in theatrical poses, and her part in *Sirens on the Wind* was mentioned. One enterprising reporter had even managed to get hold of a nude pose; maybe Kalman, her agent, had been cooperative. Some papers had included a blow-up of Dora Brown with Doug's arm around her shoulders. The heaviest of the 'heavies' had been content with a shot of the exterior of the club.

It was quite clear after a brief inspection that the editors, with one exception, had found themselves long on pictures and short of text. Chief Superintendent Freeman had given very little away. But Brel saw with anger that one very reputable Sunday — the one featuring the picture of the club — was carrying the story of Sally-Ann's appearance at Gerald's stag party.

He read the piece as he walked back to the flat, the heavy bundle of papers under his arm. It was surprisingly accurate, so accurate in fact that it was difficult to believe the source of the information had not been present at the party. Which suggested that one of Gerald's supposed friends had been happy to do him dirt. But who? Sally-Ann's body hadn't been found till lunch-time yesterday. Which of the guests had been aware of that dramatic development in time to see the relevance of the party, and tell the paper about it in the course of the afternoon or evening?

Brel was letting himself into his flat when the flaw in his reasoning struck him. Someone else would know exactly what had happened — the chap who had organized the whole thing, and he need not have been a guest at the party at all.

Brel had no chance to ponder this idea. Voices were coming from his living-room. He swung the door open and regarded the scene. Gerald, still in pyjamas and dressing-gown, was sitting on the sofa. He looked tense and nervous, the stubble on his chin giving him an air of disreputability. Opposite him Chief Superintendent Freeman's huge bulk filled an armchair and his personality filled the room. As always, Sergeant Anderson, sitting at the side of the room and busy with his notebook, was so unobtrusive that Brel scarcely noticed him.

'Good morning!'

Freeman looked up, irritated by the interruption. But Brel, annoyed to find his flat occupied in this apparently peremptory fashion, stared him out.

'Ah, Dr Breland.' The Chief Superintendent knew when to be diplomatic. 'My apologies for intruding on you like this. I got your messages last night, but too late to take any action on them. I came as soon as I could.'

Brel took a deep breath, and decided to play it equally coolly. He smiled blandly at the Chief Superintendent, and turned to Gerald.

'Have you had any breakfast?'

'N—no. Not yet.'

'Coffee?'

'No.'

'For heaven's sake! At least you can have that. What about you, Chief Superintendent? Coffee?'

'That would be very pleasant. Thanks.'

Sergeant Anderson nodded his thanks too, and Brel dumped the newspapers he'd brought in with him on to the sofa beside Gerald, and handed the top one to Freeman. 'You can read these in the interval. I shan't be long.'

In fact he was very quick. On his return, with a pot of coffee, four mugs and some buttered toast for Gerald, he found the three men reading the papers. Freeman put his aside as Brel came into the room, saying, 'I glanced through them before I left the office.' He had clearly taken Brel's interruption with good grace, from which Brel surmised that the police still wanted cooperation rather than confrontation. He hid his relief.

'I'm sure you saw that Miss Belmont's appearance at the stag party got into the press, Chief Superintendent,' he said. 'Was that your doing?'

'Most certainly not.' Freeman raised his eyebrows in surprise. But his mind was on other things. 'Mr Hinton was helping us to clarify one or two points when you returned, Doctor. I'm sure you won't mind if we carry on.'

'Of course not.'

Gerald said, 'You wanted to know when I'd gone up to my room, and I told you that I hadn't gone there, or anywhere else on the third floor, not until after poor Mrs Brown's body was found, and after you'd interviewed me. Don't you remember? You herded us all into a room, and saw us one by one—Brel was first.' Gerald bit into a piece of toast.

'Would it surprise you to learn that Mr Terence Dale

states that he heard sounds—he won't be more specific than that—coming from your room not long after you left the party in pursuit of Miss Belmont. The Dale brothers were in the twin room next to yours that night, you recall.'

'What do you expect me to say to that? In the first place, it wasnt me making any noises then, and in the second it would surprise me.'

'You've spoken to Terry Dale?' Brel said.

'Yes, Dr Breland. It was you who told us he knew Miss Belmont. He confirmed their—their relationship, told us about the flat, and about meeting you there yesterday morning. You were returning the evening bag that a maid found under Mr Hinton's bed at the club, I assume.'

'That's right,' said Brel. 'I was going to tell you about that when Forsyth interrupted us in the afternoon. The bag and her name and address and her keys in it—which is why Gerald didn't deny all knowledge of it at once—when Roberts, the porter, first showed it to him. It was the only lead he had to her whereabouts, and he was very anxious to get in touch with her, as you know.'

'Yes, I see,' said the Chief Superintendent. 'But in the event, he didn't try to get in touch with her. You went in his place, Doctor.'

'I had to go down to the country to visit my—my fiancée.'

There was a pause while everyone absorbed the weakness of this reply. Then Freeman said, 'And of course all this time Miss Belmont was dead, stuffed in that ventilation shaft, just outside the window of the room you'd been occupying.'

Gerald pushed away his second piece of toast. 'I didn't kill her,' he said. 'If you're going to accuse me, I want to call my solicitor.'

'I'm not accusing you, Mr Hinton. I've made no attempt to give you an official caution. We're merely discussing the facts, and you're amplifying your earlier statement. Miss Belmont was stabbed with the dagger from that display case, near where you admit waiting for her. She was wrapped in a club blanket, and the extra one's missing from your room. There are scratch marks on the sill of your room as if someone's been climbing in and out of the window. There may possibly be a spot or two of blood on the carpet under the window, though we're not sure about that yet. Her bag was found under your bed. And you had a motive of sorts, Mr Hinton.'

Gerald, white-faced, was suddenly aggressive. 'So why the hell haven't you warned me and arrested me?' he demanded. 'You've made out a pretty good case. But if you're waiting to prove I knew the girl, had an affair with her, you've got a damned long wait coming.'

'Mr Hinton, please, you're way ahead of me.' The Chief Superintendent was fully aware of the thin ice he was treading, and he held up a large, admonishing hand. 'I've no intention of arresting you. But I was going to ask you if you'd be good enough to come along to the Yard with me—'

'Now look here, Chief Superintendent,' Brel intervened. 'If you're going to take him away—'

'It's only while we get a formal statement typed up properly.'

'And when I've signed it I can go?'

'We'll send you back in a car.' The Chief Superintendent smiled reassuringly, then spoiled the effect a little by adding, 'Incidentally, would you let Sergeant Anderson have the suit and the shoes you were wearing on Thursday night—your evening things. You do have them here with you?'

Gerald nodded. 'Yes, I took everything with me down to the country for the weekend.' His anger had gone, and he swallowed hard, as if resigning himself to the inevitable.

As if from nowhere Sergeant Anderson produced a large plastic bag. 'Shall I get them for you, sir?'

'I'll come. I've got to dress. I suppose I'm allowed to do that,' Gerald said hoarsely.

As he followed Gerald from the room the Sergeant handed Brel some pages of typescript. 'The statement you made yesterday, sir. If you'd read it, initial each page and sign it at the end, please.'

'Certainly.' Brel was curt.

He exchanged speculative glances with Freeman. He had listened very attentively to the interview and he had sensed that, in spite of the mass of circumstantial evidence, Freeman was far from happy with the case against Gerald.

As if reading Brel's thoughts, the Chief Superintendent said, 'It's neat, almost too neat, Doctor. Belmont storms out of party. Hinton follows her, hovers outside cloakroom. By the way, Lady Wander corroborates that. Hinton takes dagger from case, persuades Belmont to go to his room, kills her, wraps her in blanket, leaves her while he returns dagger to showcase as best way of hiding it. Dora Brown sees him, so he has to stab her too and chuck her body in the bath. Later, much later, when he eventually gets back to his room, he stuffs Belmont in the shaft. Neat, yes?'

'Perhaps that's how you're expected to reason,' Brel said.

'Could be.' Freeman hesitated. 'Could be, but killers aren't often that subtle.'

'You said yourself it was almost too neat. And you didn't mention the neat motive someone provided for Gerald first.'

The Chief Superintendent rose to his feet. He shrugged, yawned and apologized. 'I didn't get much sleep last night. We tried a little experiment — the sort of thing the French always seem to do. We re-enacted the two murders, just as I've described them, with police officers playing the parts. We even broke another vase — a cheap one this time. We guessed Dora Brown knocked it over as she backed away from the killer. It was quite illuminating.'

'How?'

'For one thing, the time element. It was surprising how quickly it could have been done, if the disposal of the Belmont girl's body was left till later — well within the time available to Mr Hinton.'

'Didn't you find anything in his favour? He's quite tall, but he's not a big man, and —'

'Quite. An officer who is much the same build had great difficulty coping with the girl playing Miss Belmont, though he did succeed in the end. It would have been even harder with a really dead weight.'

'Was that all?' Brel was disappointed.

'No. Mr Dale swears he heard no sounds at what would have been the relevant time, but only much earlier. There's also the odd point that though Mr Hinton delayed going after Miss Belmont, he was able to see her disappearing into that cloakroom cul-de-sac. She must have moved very slowly — and one wonders why.'

The Chief Superintendent broke off as Gerald and Sergeant Anderson returned. 'Ready? Good.' He turned to Brel. 'Thanks a lot, Dr Breland. Incidentally, there shouldn't be any trouble for Mrs Cain over this affair. Her brother — Sullivan, the junkie who just came out of jail — he's in the clear. He's got an unshakable alibi for Thursday night. So we can count him out.'

Brel nodded absently. He'd entirely forgotten about Tom Sullivan. Once Sally-Ann Belmont's body had been found, Dora Brown's swap with Myrtle Cain had no longer seemed relevant.

The immediate problem, however, was Gerald. Brel was not entirely sure about Freeman's intentions. He found a set of spare keys for Gerald in case he wasn't at home when his friend returned, and he intervened again before he let him depart with the two policemen.

'You're happy about this, Gerald? Shall   come with you? Or could I phone your lawyer? Or mine? Or I've got a patient who specializes in criminal cases.'

Freeman remained silent, and Gerald hesitated. 'No,' he said finally. 'Not at this stage. I'll trust them,' nodding at the Chief Superintendent and the Sergeant. 'I'm innocent. What have I got to lose?'

Possibly a great deal, Brel thought, but Freeman smiled amiably and Brel let them go.

In fact, he was glad to be alone. There was only a little time before he must set off for Sir Richard Wander's and he wanted to consider the implications of Freeman's comments. He knew now, or he thought he knew, some of the questions that had to be asked if the killer were ever to be traced.

Sir Richard Wander himself opened the front door of his Belgravia house. He ushered Brel across an imposing hall into a room he called the library, though most of the leather-bound books looked unread, and asked him what he'd have to drink.

'Whisky, please,' Brel said. 'Thank you,' he added quickly as he saw the amount that was being poured. 'No. No ice. A little soda.' He waited for Wander to open the conversation and explain his unexpected invitation.

Sir Richard seemed in no hurry. He gave himself a very dark scotch, waved Brel to a leather armchair and sat down opposite him, taking a long pull at his drink. 'Dreadful business, this,' he said eventually. 'Dreadful business. Jenson phoned me as soon as he got the chance. He's a good man, Jenson. Excellent club secretary.'

'Very efficient,' Brel agreed.

'It was thanks to me he got the job, and he's grateful.

Always keeps me in touch with things.'

'And why not?' said Brel. 'You're the Chairman of the Management Committee.'

'Yes.' Sir Richard paused, glancing round the room. Suddenly he stood up. 'Breland—ever heard of the Gresley Hotel off Curzon Street?'

'No. Should I have?' Brel was slightly taken aback by this sudden change of subject.

Wander shrugged. 'Don't know. You might. It's quite a small place, very select, but it doesn't exactly cater for family parties, if you know what I mean.'

Brel nodded slowly. He could imagine the establishment, its reputation safeguarded by its patrons, businessmen with their secretaries, wives with their boyfriends, husbands with other people's wives.

Wander went on. 'Look, Breland, you're a man of the world—and a doctor. I take it I can rely on your discretion.'

Brel hesitated. 'Well, yes,' he said, 'but I can't be a party to—'

'Oh, it's not like that,' said Wander. 'I've got to tell someone—get some advice—and you seem to be in with the police. I didn't kill anyone, but I did know Sally-Ann. She was a very attractive girl, not a great actress, but adequate. My wife had been in the States for weeks. Her mother was ill. You understand, some men are highly—'

'Sally-Ann Belmont?' Brel stared at Sir Richard in amazement. 'You took the Belmont girl to the Gresley?'

Wander smoothed the hair over his balding head in a nervous gesture. 'Yes, damn it. If I'd known she was going to get herself murdered in my club, it's the last thing I'd have done, but—' He broke off, finished his drink and got up to pour himself another. He gestured towards Brel's glass but Brel shook his head. 'It was pretty brief and casual. I gave her a nice present when my wife came home, and I promised I'd get her a West End part.

Which I did, in *Sirens*. It wasn't a big part, but now I
wish to God I hadn't done that either. The management'll remember how it came about. And with her
getting killed in the club, there could be a nasty little
scandal, and that's the last thing I want at the moment.'

'Your wife?' Brel said tentatively.

'No, not entirely. She wouldn't like it, that's true. But
there's something more important.' Wander leant
forward in his chair. 'You understand, this is really
confidential — just between the two of us, eh Breland?'

'Like everything you've told me, Sir Richard.'

'Yes, but this —' Wander took a deep breath. 'In the
first place, there's a lot of money involved. There's a
takeover in prospect, and I can't alienate any
shareholders. Then there's another point — I've been
given reason to suppose my name will appear in the next
Honours List. And that could help me in the City, too. A
sordid scandal could ruin everything.'

Brel nodded solemnly. For a moment, he dared not
speak. He was afraid that if he opened his mouth he'd
explode with laughter — or anger, when he remembered
Gerald.

He recovered his composure, and knew there was only
one question he could reasonably ask: 'Why are you
telling me all this, Sir Richard?'

'It's obvious, Breland. I want you to help me. Actually,
it was Alan Jenson who suggested you might. He said you
seemed to be well in with the police. And what I need is
some warning. Clearly they don't know anything about
my little affair with Miss Belmont yet, but if they do get
on to it, it might be hushed up — if I knew in time. After
all, it's not relevant to the murders. You see the point.
Just let me know if you hear anything. I thought it would
help if you knew what to look out for.'

'I understand, Sir Richard,' Brel said. He put his half-

finished glass down on a table and got to his feet. 'I must
go.'

'Yes. Yes, of course. And thank you, Breland. I'll hope
to repay your understanding one of these days.'

Brel took his leave. As a doctor he'd seen many facets of
human nature, some dreadful, some magnificent, and
he'd thought he was beyond the usual reactions. But
Wander's attitude to two deaths, including that of a girl
he's slept with more than once, still seemed vaguely
disgusting. He walked back to his car slowly. The reasons
for Wander's confidences seemed clear enough; given
adequate warning, it was by no means impossible that he
could exert pressure in the right quarters.

But Sir Richard might have said, or implied, more
than he intended.

CHAPTER 14

'Here we are, sir.'

The police car, an unmarked black Rover, drew up at
the kerb. The driver leapt out and opened the door.
Gerald Hinton got out more slowly. He felt old and
mentally battered, though in fact he had only been kept
at the Yard for a couple of hours and had been treated
with every courtesy. Nevertheless, the repetitive questions
had been a strain, and he stumbled a little as he crossed
the pavement to the front door of the Harley Street
House.

'Thank you,' he called over his shoulder to the driver,
who watched him find his key before moving off.

He was unaccustomed to the lock, and it irritated him.
He wondered in amazement how his life could have
changed so drastically in five days. Last Wednesday,
when he left home for London, he had been a relatively

happy man, his only problem the Lydneys' vague, unstated disapproval of the forthcoming wedding. Even that, he had been sure, would pass once he and Elizabeth were married and the first grandchild in evidence. Now, the present was hideous and the future offered no hope of improvement.

Gerald let himself into the flat. In the living-room, he flung himself into a chair and stared straight in front of him. He was glad Brel wasn't back yet. He was immensely grateful to Brel, but at the moment the last thing he wanted was company. He sat for some while. The telephone rang and he tried to ignore it. But when the rings persisted, he rose reluctantly and went to answer it.

'Brel?'

'I'm sorry. Dr Breland's not here at present.'

'That's Gerald, isn't it? It's Jack—Jack Dawson—here. I was calling Brel about you. Marjorie and I have been worried. Are you okay?'

'Yes. They haven't arrested me yet, if that's what you mean. Actually I don't even have to stay in London. Freeman—the Detective Chief Superintendent who seems to be in charge of the case—says I can go where I like, as long as I keep the police informed of my whereabouts. I said I'd go home tomorrow morning. After all, there's work to be done at the plant. Not that it matters so much now.'

'Why's that?'

'I doubt if I'm going away at the end of the month—unless it's to prison. The wedding may be off.'

'Off? Hell, Gerald! Hang on.' There was confused muttering at the other end of the line and then Jack Dawson's voice again. 'Come and have supper with us tonight, you and Brel, about eight.'

'Well, I'm not sure—'

'Why not? Marjorie says you must.'

'I'll check with Brel when he comes in and let you know.'

Sighing, Gerald put down the receiver. He wished he were back at home, but he hadn't the energy to do anything about it. He couldn't face a long, slow drive on Sunday roads. Besides, it might be as well to continue to compare notes with Brel. If that meant another night in London — so be it, he thought resignedly.

Brel's return did something to relieve his depression. While Brel prepared an omelette and a salad for a late lunch, Gerald laid the table and recounted his experiences at Scotland Yard.

'They seemed to ask the same things over and over again,' he said. 'I suppose they were trying to catch me out. But sometimes they'd come up with a new twist, and hammer away at that.'

'What sort of twists?' Brel asked, folding the omelette over the mushrooms.

'Well, one thing was how I could have seen the Belmont girl go into the ladies' cloakroom unless I'd gone after her immediately.'

'Yes, I know,' said Brel. I've been thinking about that too. Freeman mentioned it to me. It's an interesting point — a question of timing.'

Gerald stared at him. 'Interesting! It may be interesting for you,' he exploded, 'but it's utter bloody nonsense as far as I'm concerned. All I know is that when I came out of the Irving Room I could see her. I wasn't thinking about timing, or any other damn thing except talking to her. Look,' he said, 'I'm sorry, but can't we talk about something else? I've had enough of Sally-Ann Belmont for one morning. What did Wander want with you?'

Brel did his best to make his interview with Sir Richard sound amusing, without breaking any confidences. He didn't mention the Gresley Hotel episodes, but emphasized Wander's eagerness for warning of anything that might lead to scandal. Gradually Gerald relaxed. He even managed to eat a good meal.

'Wander should have my problems,' he said finally.

'They'll pass, Gerald. They must. Try not to worry.' Brel grinned hopefully as he finished his cheese. 'Coffee?'

'Please.' Gerald paused. 'While you were out I had Jack Dawson on the phone. Marjorie's asked us to supper tonight. I don't know that I—'

'Splendid!' interrupted Brel. 'I think that's a good idea. Let's go.'

'I'll have to call them back and tell them.'

'Fine. You do that while I make some coffee.'

Gerald went to the phone a little reluctantly. But he couldn't blame Brel. At least it would make the evening pass. He dialled the Dawsons' number.

'Who's that?' Jack Dawson said abruptly.

Gerald was startled. 'It's me—Gerald. What's the matter?'

'Oh. Sorry. Terribly sorry.' Dawson's voice lost its harshness. 'I—I thought— The fact, is, Gerald, we've just had a most unpleasant phone call. Unfortunately Marjorie took it, and she's pretty upset. Some bugger! I could break his neck!'

'D'you mean an obscene call?' Gerald found it hard to understand such a strong reaction on Marjorie's part.

'Not exactly obscene, in the usual sense. The plain fact is, Gerald, it was about you. He—it was a man—said that Marjorie and I, as your closest friends, ought to keep an eye on you. Now that, instead of getting married to Elizabeth, you were going to be charged with murder, you might be tempted to—to do something silly.'

'Like what? Kill myself?'

'Yes.'

Gerald's shocked silence must have lasted twenty seconds. Then, 'Are you there? Are you all right?' Jack's voice sounded in his ear, suddenly anxious.

'Yes, I'm here.' Gerald made an effort, but his words sounded like ice particles. He said the first thing that came into his head. 'Tell Marjorie how sorry I am, will you, Jack?'

'You've got nothing to be sorry for,' Dawson said firmly, now in control of his temper. 'If there's any more of this nonsense we'll report it to the police, though heaven knows what they can do. He was speaking from a call-box, Marjorie says, and she'd never heard his voice, to her knowledge. Apparently it sounded funny—a handkerchief or something over the mouthpiece, I suppose. Now, what about tonight? You're coming, I hope.'

'Yes, if—'

'Fine. We'll see you and Brel about eight, then. We can all have a good talk.'

'Thanks a lot,' Gerald said quietly.

He turned as Brel came into the living-room with two cups of coffee on a tray. He felt physically sick, but was unaware that the colour had drained completely from his face.

Brel took one look at him and acted instinctively. He put down the tray, sat Gerald on a chair, grabbed at his pulse and pushed his head down between his knees. It was only a minute or two before Gerald had recovered sufficiently to sip at the glass of brandy Brel was holding out to him.

'What brought that on?' asked Brel. 'Something Jack said?'

Gerald told him, and added, 'You don't seem all that surprised, Brel. I suppose not. I suppose I should have expected it. One's always reading about people getting crank calls, even in the most hideous of circumstances. But why the Dawsons? How would he know they were friends of mine? Their name's not in any of the papers, is it? Nor Elizabeth's?'

'I don't think so,' Brel said absently. He was by no means certain that this was just a crank call. It could well have come from the hoaxer, the murderer. But why? Gerald was far too tough a character to contemplate suicide. It could only be another smear. But again, why?

After lunch, on the pretext that he'd slept badly the night before, Gerald went to his room to rest. In fact, he felt he needed to be alone though, lying on his bed, he found himself dozing fitfully. Brel had asked him for the Lydneys' number and from time to time he was aware of what seemed to be a interminable phone call. He ignored it.

Actually Brel was making a succession of calls. A more thorough study of the Sunday papers had confirmed his impression that none of them mentioned the Dawsons or Elizabeth Lydney. Even the story on the stag party hadn't given the name of Gerald's finacée. It all confirmed a theory that had begun to form in his mind, and was seeming more and more plausible as one piece of evidence was added to another.

Brel started from the assumption that Gerald was innocent, both of the murders and of the paternity of Sally-Ann Belmont's unborn child. This being so, Brel argued that someone must be totally committed to the persecution of Gerald. All the indications were that this someone knew a great deal about Gerald, and hated him, whatever he might claim about his lack of enemies. What was more, it was fairly clear that the original intention had been to frame him for Sally-Ann's murder. Dora Brown's death must have been incidental, an unforeseen necessity.

It was inconceivable that Sally-Ann had connived at her own death. Therefore, she had been used. Probably persuaded that she was helping to play some kind of practical joke, she had merely followed instructions — a script—on the night of Gerald's party. After her dramatic departure from the Irving Room she had purposely delayed, in the hope that he would follow and could be led towards the ladies' cloakroom. There, he might well be seen waiting outside by the display case, while she slipped away through the service door and passages. Then, still following her directions, she went upstairs to meet her—her producer, probably in a bedroom on the third floor, where she was killed in cold blood, and afterwards stuffed into the ventilation shaft. It was her death, not her accusation, that was intended to be Gerald's undoing. Her accusation merely provided a credible motive.

In between calls, Brel considered his argument yet again. It was all supposition, of course, but he could spot no logical flaws. A lot had depended on Gerald's decision to chase after Sally-Ann, but it was a reaction that could reasonably have been expected. And even if he'd failed to do so, it would not necessarily have been disastrous. The plan had been devised with a great deal of ingenuity and cunning.

Waiting for the phone to be answered, Brel considered the list of prospects he'd prepared. It had started at the most elementary level with the fourteen people at Gerald's party, plus a possible outside hoaxer. He had immediately crossed off himself, Gerald and Jack Dawson. Four more names had been easily eliminated. They belonged to men who neither lived nor worked in London, who weren't familiar with the Arts and Letters Club, and who seemingly had had no means of knowing exactly when Sally-Ann's body was discovered and thus providing timely information on Gerald's party for the morning paper.

Of the others on his list, Brel had discovered that one had gone abroad on business on the Friday, and another was in bed with gastro-enteritis, for which his wife seemed to blame Gerald and the club's food; Brel suspected that the man's doctor had tactfully attributed the results of overeating and too much alcohol to a bug. Yet another was an unlikely starter—he was excessively fat and slow-moving, and as far as Brel knew had only been invited at the last moment to make fourteen.

He was left with Charles Lydney, Ryle, the Dales—and the possible hoaxer. It was the Lydney household that he was ringing now with some reluctance.

'Hello! Hello!' a voice said finally.

'Mrs Lydney?'

'Yes, speaking. Who's that?'

'This is Dr Breland, Mrs Lydney. You remember?'

'Yes. What is it? What do you want?'

'It's very simple, Mrs Lydney. I wonder if you could answer what may seem a rather stupid question. Has either Charles or Nick been out since we all met yesterday?'

'Been out? Do you mean out of the house, the garden? No. We all went to church at eleven, but that's all. They're down by the swimming-pool now. Do you want to speak to them?'

'No, thank you, Mrs Lydney. Thank you again. Goodbye.'

Hastily Brel cut the connection. Then he crossed Charles and Ryle off his list. The Dawsons' call had come from a call-box, and it was a fair assumption that a lengthy call to a newspaper spilling the beans about Gerald's party wouldn't have been made from inside the house, where it might have been overheard.

He hesitated before dialling the Dales. He didn't share Gerald's faith that in no circumstances would the Dales plot to throw blame on him. On the other hand, he was as sure as he could be that they hadn't planned Sally-Ann Belmont's appearance. Therefore they didn't fill the bill if her performance was only a preliminary to the main event of the evening—the killing. And he was becoming more and more attached to that theory.

Nevertheless, they should be crossed off the list. He dialled and Peter Dale answered almost at once. As soon as he learnt that Brel was the caller he became voluble. All Brel had to do was listen and, with a little prompting, his questions were answered before they were asked. In fact, Peter Dale was in a state of agitation and anxiety, and was happy to pour out his troubles to someone who he thought would sympathize.

It seemed that the two Dale brothers and their wives had been together in Terry Dale's house early on Saturday evening, when the police had called to announce that Sally-Ann Belmont had been murdered, and to take preliminary statements. Though the police had been discreet in their questions, as soon as they had gone Jennifer had continued with her own interrogation. It was not long before she had discovered the truth about Terry's relationship with Sally-Ann. There had been an almightly row, and Terry had been ordered out of the house.

'Then blow me if Susan didn't decide to act up,' Peter said sadly. 'She refused to let Terry come home with us. She said I could choose between her and my brother. So Terry came with me, and Susan stayed with Jennifer. He's still here—dead drunk. I can tell you we really laid one on last night, once we were alone. A ghastly mess all round.'

'Have you seen the Sunday papers yet?' Brel asked.

Peter groaned. 'No. We have a couple delivered, but as far as I know they're still sitting on the doorstep.' He paused. 'Christ! I never thought of that. I suppose the Belmont murder's made the press.'

'Of course. It's a lead story.'

'God! I hope it gets cleared up soon. If the reporters ferret out Terry's connection with the girl and it becomes public, Jenny'll never forgive him. It's not been mentioned yet, has it?'

'I don't think so, and I went through the papers pretty carefully.' Brel thought briefly of Sir Richard Wander. The number of people who had a vested interest in hushing up various aspects of the affair was growing rapidly. 'Thanks a lot, Peter. I must go. Goodbye.'

'But you haven't told me why you phoned —'

Brel put down the receiver. Unless Peter was a brilliant actor he was responsible neither for the account of Gerald's stag party in the newspaper, nor for the call to the Dawsons. And a dead drunk Terry seemed equally in the clear. Brel put lines through each of their names. Only the hoaxer remained.

The hoaxer — whom Brel now equated with the killer — was unnamed, except very tentatively in Brel's mind. All he had, Brel knew, was suspicions, straws in the wind. Chief Superintendent Freeman would probably laugh at them, and at the rather pathetic enquiries he'd been able to make. He'd formed a theory and sought evidence to support it. It could be argued that he'd found nothing to negate his theory, but he was no nearer proving it.

As he heard Gerald come out of the spare room and go along to the bathroom, Brel tore up his list into very small pieces, and dropped them into the wastepaper basket. His afternoon's work had been merely an exercise in futility.

Before he went to bed that night, after a pleasant but fruitless evening at the Dawsons', Brel reached a decision. He was a doctor, not a detective, not some kind of private eye. Admittedly he was Gerald Hinton's friend, and he would stand by Gerald to the best of his ability, but theories and enquiries should be left to the authorities. He must not meddle in what was strictly none of his business.

CHAPTER 15

Brel slept relatively happily on this decision. But the next morning, when the time came to say goodbye to Gerald, he began to have second thoughts.

Gerald wasn't unduly effusive—it wasn't in his nature—but he was clearly deeply affected by the events of the past few days and by his friend's support. 'Thanks, Brel,' he said as he left. 'Thanks for putting up with me and—and everything. Many wouldn't have. I'm most grateful.'

'Forget it. If there's anything else I can do . . .'

On and off throughout the day Brel recalled his words. He told himself that his half-finished sentence was merely a trite expression, and in no way a promise of any kind of commitment to Gerald. Nevertheless, the situation nagged at him like a sore tooth.

Mondays always tended to be busy in a doctor's practice, as many patients waited until the weekend was over before phoning about their ailments and demanding appointments. This Monday was particularly so, for Dr Aymer, the middle partner, had taken his family on holiday, and his work had to be divided between his two colleagues.

Dr Farre, who had heavy social engagements later in the week, decided to be on call on both Monday and Tuesday nights, so Brel found himself unexpectedly free. He considered going for a walk in Regent's Park or strolling along to one of the local pubs or staying at home and doing absolutely nothing. In the end, as he had known he would, he made his way to the Arts and Letters Club.

The place looked strangely desolate. He had wondered

if it would be besieged by a crowd of pressmen and photographers, but they had evidently come and gone. A uniformed constable, standing inside the door, checked his name against a list of members—non-members had to state their business—and he was allowed past.

'Good evening, sir.' Roberts greeted him from the porter's box and came out into the hall. 'We're very quiet today, at least so far as members are concerned, and I'm afraid the dining-room's closed.'

'Why's that?'

'Well, the staff have been so busy answering questions and making statements, and there are so few members around, that Mr Jenson decided it wasn't worth while doing a proper meal this evening. But the bar's open, and they're serving pre-theatre snacks there, as usual.'

'Thanks.'

Brel didn't go immediately to the bar. Instead, he went up in the lift to the Irving Room—the room where Gerald's ill-fated party had been held. Standing outside its double doors he looked towards the corridor leading to the ladies' cloakroom. It was no more than thirty feet away.

As Brel had suspected, the Chief Superintendent had understated the case. For Gerald to see her after his slightly delayed attempt at pursuit, Sally-Ann Belmont hadn't just moved slowly along the passage. She must have deliberately loitered, presumably so that she should remain in view.

Brel walked along the cul-de-sac that led only to the ladies', and was about to turn back when he heard his name called. Myrtle Cain had come out of the cloakroom.

'Hello, Mrs Cain. I didn't expect to see you here.'

'The police let us in this morning, Doctor. The—the dressing-room's locked, of course. Not that anyone would want to use it so soon after poor Dora being found there. But otherwise—apart from so few members around—

we're in business as usual.'

'Good.'

Although they were alone in the passage Myrtle Cain came close to Brel and lowered her voice. 'I wanted to say thank you, Doctor, for arranging things with the police for me. The Superintendent was very kind and understanding.'

Brel smiled at her. 'I didn't really do anything. But you must be relieved to know your brother wasn't involved at all.'

'Yes, indeed. It's wonderful. Mind you, I still feel guilty about Dora. If I'd not changed shifts with her she'd be alive now.'

'But you'd be dead,' Brel said gently.

To his surprise Mrs Cain shook her head firmly. 'No, I'd not have been here in the ladies' then, not at the time the Super said Dora got herself killed. I'd have been in the staff canteen, having my supper. I can't understand why Dora wasn't there. It's always a good meal in the evenings, just the same as the members get, a real perk.'

Brel checked his rising excitement. 'You never said anything about this before, Mrs Cain,' he said levelly. 'Why not?'

'How was I to know she'd got killed in our supper-time?' Myrtle Cain was indignant. 'Not until Superintendent Freeman told me.'

At once Brel was placatory. 'No, of course not,' he said. He thought again; Poor Dora. In the first place, she shouldn't have been on duty on Thursday evening at all, and in the second she ought to have been in the canteen when the killer replaced the dagger. It was bad luck for her — and for the killer.

'He told me about the door not being locked, too,' Mrs Cain volunteered. 'I had wondered.'

'You mean the door of the display cabinet where the dagger was kept?' Brel frowned. 'I thought it was just carelessness on the part of whoever dusts inside it. Wasn't it often left unlocked?'

'That's not true, Doctor. I know the lady who does the cleaning and she's very particular. Mind you,' Myrtle Cain conceded, 'anyone can make a mistake once. But that wasn't what I was talking about. I meant the dressing-room door.'

'The dressing-room?'

'Where you found Dora. Look, Doctor, it's like this. If ladies change in the evenings and leave their things in one of the dressing-rooms, they're supposed to lock it when then leave and take the key with them. Dora gave Mrs Sencourt the key, and it was still in her evening bag later. But she can't remember — Mrs Sencourt, that is — whether she locked the door after her. She thinks she did, because all her day clothes were there, and quite a lot of things she'd bought. But she's not sure. Or at least that's what the Super told me.'

'That's very interesting,' Brel said.

And he meant it. He was intrigued by the information that Mrs Cain had produced so casually, and it confirmed his faith in the Chief Superintendent. Freeman wasn't taking the easy way out, and assuming Gerald's guilt. He was continuing with his enquiries, digging deep, and possibly — just possibly — his train of thought was running parallel with Brel's own.

'Good evening, Dr Breland. Good evening, Myrtle. Everything in order?'

Startled, Brel swung round. He hadn't heard footsteps on the carpeted corridor, and was unaware that anyone had come up behind them. Feeling vaguely guilty at being caught talking to the ladies' cloakroom attendant, he said hurriedly, 'Oh hello. I was asking Mrs Cain about Doug Brown,' and at once wished he hadn't felt it necessary to explain himself.

Alan Jenson seemed to notice nothing unusual. He

merely smiled and said, 'Doug Brown, yes. Isn't it good news that he's in the clear?' He sounded genuinely pleased.

'Yes, indeed,' Brel said, remembering the unexpected interest the secretary had taken in young Brown.

'And he's got a job, Mr Jenson,' Myrtle Cain added with satisfaction. 'I was just telling the doctor here. Someone Dora used to work for saw about her death in the paper, and about Doug being unemployed, and asked him if he'd like to be a kind of odd-job man and porter at a sort of hotel he owns.'

'Splendid,' the secretary said. 'I hope he's going to make a real effort to go straight now.'

'I'm sure he is, Mr Jenson. This has all been a dreadful shock for him. He was very fond of his mother.'

'What hotel is this?'

Brel almost held his breath as he waited for an answer to his question. Without any justification at all, he had at once thought of the Gresley. But he was wrong. The hotel, Myrtle Cain explained, was more of a hostel or lodging-house than a real hotel. Most of its rooms were occupied on long lets by students, because it was very convenient for the London School of Economics off the Aldwych.

Her explanation was interrupted by the arrival of two ladies, and Brel took the opportunity to depart. He went down to the bar and bought himself a whisky. He considered a snack but, after an almost non-existent lunch, was not particularly tempted by a mere toasted sandwich for supper.

When he had finished his drink he went in search of the Chief Superintendent, but neither Freeman nor Sergeant Anderson were in the club. A detective-constable — the sole occupant of the smoking-room the police had taken over as their temporary headquarters — was polite but not forthcoming as to their whereabouts, though he volunteered to take any messages.

Leaving the club, Brel returned to his car, where he sat for some time studying the London street guide he always kept in the glove compartment. The street Myrtle Cain had given as the location of Doug Brown's new place of work was short and narrow and hard to find without a magnifying-glass.

However, when Brel had finally tracked it down, it didn't take him long to reach it. He parked firmly in a 'No Parking' zone directly opposite his destination, a rather seedy-looking building that described itself as a private hotel. Inside, the hall was tidy and clean. Two youths were sitting on the bottom of the stairs. He recognized one as Doug Brown.

'Hello, Doug,' he said. 'My name's Dr Breland. Can I have a word with you?'

'What about?' Brown got to his feet, suddenly wary. 'What do you want?'

The other youth stood up too. 'I'll be off then, Doug. See you later. Don't forget.' He nodded curiously at Brel and took the stairs two at a time.

'I won't,' Doug shouted after him.

'Enjoying your job?' Brel said. 'Found a friend.'

'Maybe. What's it to you?' Brown challenged. 'You were at that bleeding club the night my ma was killed. I saw you. You're not fuzz, though.'

'No, I'm nothing to do with the police, Doug,' Brel said gently. 'I told you who I am. My name's Breland. Dr Breland. I more or less found your mother—'

'So—'

'If it's any consolation to you, she died quickly,' Brel said. 'She didn't suffer at all.' He saw Doug's prominent Adam's apple work up and down as the short, burly young man tried to swallow his feelings, and he seized his chance. 'She was a sick woman, your mother, wasn't she? Under a doctor's care?'

'She went to the outpatients at the hospital and had some tests. They gave her pills, like, and put her on a diet. It didn't do much good. The pills made her depressed.' Doug said gruffly, his aggression temporarily forgotten.

'But this diet? It was salt-free, I imagine, and pretty strict. Is that why she didn't have supper in the staff canteen at the club? Did she take sandwiches instead?'

'What if she did?' Doug took the question as an accusation. 'What's it matter? She's dead now, isn't she? That bleeder Jenson can't sack her for breaking his piddling little rules.'

'You mean she did take sandwiches, but never told anyone because she was afraid Jenson would hear about it.'

'That's right. She thought he'd be annoyed. Eating sandwiches in the ladies'. Leaving crumbs on the floor. What about mice?' Doug Brown was mimicking the secretary's tone, and Brel found himself grinning. The grin seemed to encourage Doug and he went on, 'It was only lately she started taking her own supper, after they told her off at the out-patients for breaking her diet. It was the salt,' he ended miserably. 'She wasn't meant to eat no salt.'

'Thanks. That's all I wanted to know.' Brel took a five-pound note from his wallet and handed it to Doug. 'You sounded as if you were going out later tonight. Perhaps this'll help the party.'

Doug Brown's face expressed amazement. 'Is that all you want to know?'

'Sure.'

'But why? I don't understand.'

'Medical evidence. It might help to prove who killed your mother.'

With a wave of his hand, Brel walked out of the place, pleased with his efforts. Everything pointed in the same direction. There was no doubt about means or opportunity or the necessary information. But why? What would the man gain from preventing Gerald's marriage and disgracing him. Revenge, perhaps. But for what? They were the merest acquaintances. Brel decided he must be wrong. But he couldn't stop now. He had to go on, to make absolutely certain.

Brel was in no doubt about how he was going to spend the rest of the evening. He proposed to have a long, leisurely meal, and then make his way to the theatre by the time the curtain came down on the last act of *Sirens on the Wind*. He wanted to have another talk with June Clairvale. It was more than possible that, now Sally-Ann was dead, Miss Clairvale might speak more freely about her. Anyway, it was worth a try.

The stage-door keeper was the one who had been on duty on Friday night, when Brel had been with Gerald. He recognized Brel at once. ' 'Evening, Doctor, Want to see Miss Clairvale again?'

'Yes, please.'

'She should be along any minute. They came down about ten minutes ago.' He settled himself back on his stool inside his brightly-lighted little box. 'Good house tonight,' he added.

'Really? I'd have thought — '

'You would, wouldn't you? But there's been a rush on tickets today. Everyone's been reading about *Sirens* and talking about *Sirens*, so everyone's got to see *Sirens*. Funny thing, human nature.'

'Very funny,' Brel agreed.

He was saved from any more homespun philosophy by the arrival of June Clairvale, as usual among the first of the cast to get away. She showed no surprise at seeing Brel.

Tucking her hand under his arm, she said, 'Same place as last time?'

'Why not? I liked it.'

On a Monday night it was quiet in the drinking club. The tables were half empty. No one was dancing. The accordion was being played very softly. Even the mynah bird's greeting sounded a little subdued.

When the barman had brought their drinks—another cognac for Brel and a brandy and benedictine for June Clairvale—she leaned across the table, her chin propped in one hand, and said, 'I suppose I'd be a fool to kid myself you're here because of my beautiful big eyes. You want to talk some more about Sally-Ann. That right?'

'I'm afraid so,' Brel grinned. 'It's become infinitely more important than it was, as you can imagine.'

'For your friend, Gerry?'

'It's Gerald,' Brel corrected. 'Nobody calls him Gerry. Miss Clairvale—'

'June.'

'What? Oh yes, June. June, are you sure you didn't hear Sally-Ann call her boy-friend Terry, not Gerry.'

June shrugged. 'Could be. I didn't mention it to the police, anyway.'

'They've questioned you?'

'Yes, all of us. They came backstage after the show on Saturday night. Questions. Questions. My God, I thought they'd never stop. I gave up.'

'Gave up what?'

'Trying to make them understand. They would have it Sally-Ann was promiscuous, always hopping in and out of bed with different guys. But she wasn't like that. I mayn't have known her well, but at least I knew that. Sure, she used sex to get what she wanted—expensive clothes, jewellery, things like that—but she was faithful to the chap of the moment. She wasn't any kind of nympho.' June Clairvale had become quite indignant.

'Did you know she was pregnant?'

'Yes. She had some morning sickness a couple of

months ago and she told me then. She was happy about it. Her boy-friend had promised to marry her, and that's what she'd always wanted—marriage to a rich man, every luxury, the joys of the jet set.'

Brel kept his peace. June Clairvale's description of Sally-Ann's dream sounded credible enough, but scarcely one she would have achieved with Terry Dale as her husband. Sir Richard Wander would have been much more likely to fulfil her ambitions.

A minute or two later June said, 'Poor Sally-Ann. I feel a bitch talking about her this way. I hope they get the man that killed her. When I think of the trouble she took finding that dress and stole. She said it was for a special occasion and had to be just perfect, all gold and white. I thought it was for something her boy-friend had planned.' She shook her head sadly. 'Some special occasion.'

Brel said, 'It may not have been anything to do with her current boy-friend. In fact, it probably wasn't. Tell me, June, supposing she met an old—acquaintance, let's call him—and he asked her to stage that performance at the party in return for a nice present, would she have played?'

'An old acquaintance?' June frowned. 'An ex-boy-friend, you mean?'

'Possibly. Possibly not.'

'Yes, I think she would. If she liked him, and it was a very nice present—money even or something like that, something she could think of as a professional engagement. But he wouldn't have any reason for killing her, would he? After all, she did what he wanted. Unless—'

'God knows,' Brel said. 'Better leave it to the police. They seem to know what they're doing.'

Deliberately he smothered a yawn. He'd got more than he'd hoped for from June Clairvale, and now he wanted to go. He offered to drive her home and she took the hint at once. She kissed him goodbye on the pavement outside her apartment building.

'Maybe when all this is over we might get together again,' she said, a little wistfully. 'I suppose you wouldn't like to come in now.'

'I'd love to,' Brel said. He was beginning to like June Clairvale more and more. 'But not tonight, my sweet. There are things I must do.'

It was almost midnight when Brel reached his own flat, but he paid no attention to the time. He dialled Sir Richard Wander's number and demanded to speak to him.

CHAPTER 16

Soon after ten o'clock the next morning a uniformed chauffeur arrived at Brel's Harley Street establishment, and asked to see the doctor personally. He admitted he had no formal appointment, but insisted that nevertheless he was expected. Puzzled, the housekeeper who had opened the door to him glanced at the gleaming Rolls-Royce standing at the kerb, showed him into the waiting-room and phoned upstairs to Kathleen Taylor.

Brel was busy, and his strict instructions were that when he was with a patient he was not to be interrupted, except in the direst emergency. So, after a few minutes, Kathleen came down herself to investigate. The chauffeur was polite but firm. He had a package to deliver to Dr Breland. He had been told to deliver it personally, and when his boss said personally he meant personally.

'Then you'll have to wait,' Kathleen said, a little tartly.

'If you say so, miss.' The chauffeur appeared to acquiesce. He chose a magazine from the table in the centre of the room, sat down in a corner and began to read. But, as Kathleen was opening the door, he called after her, without bothering to lift his head. 'Miss, Dr Breland is very anxious to get this package. If I were you I'd tell him about it right away.'

Kathleen didn't reply. She went out, shutting the door deliberately but gently behind her. The chauffeur looked up and grinned at the only other person in the room, a young girl, a patient of Dr Farre, who returned his grin with a blank stare. He returned to his magazine and waited.

To Kathleen's annoyance he did not have to wait unduly long. She told Brel as soon as he came into her office while his patient was dressing, and to her surprise he raced downstairs at once. Coming to an abrupt halt at the door of the waiting-room, he composed himself for a moment before going in. Four pairs of eyes focused on him.

The young girl had been replaced by a mother and child. Brel's next patient, an irascible man who hated to be kept waiting, had arrived early for his appointment and stood up hopefully. The chauffeur was already standing, about to fetch another magazine.

'Good morning.' It was a professional smile, warm and encompassing everyone, even the small boy. 'I'll be with you in a very few minutes, Colonel,' Brel said to the man, who sank back into his chair. To the chauffeur, he said, 'I'm Dr Breland. You've got a package for me.'

'Yes, sir.' He handed Brel a large brown envelope, well stuffed and sealed. 'Sir Richard asked me to get you to sign this receipt yourself.'

As the others looked on curiously, Brel signed the paper and handed it to the chauffeur. 'Thank you very much, and please thank Sir Richard for me.'

'Very good, sir.'

Upstairs again, his patient was dressed and waiting for him. Brel forced himself to concentrate, to keep his mind on medical matters, but his glance kept sliding to the envelope at the side of his desk. And as soon as possible, almost before the door had closed behind the patient and he was alone, Brel slit open the envelope and took out the contents.

He leafed quickly through the papers. They were much as he had expected: the proof of an advertisement, the clippings from newspapers in which it had appeared, a completed application form with copies of references attached to it, some correspondence and a letter from Sir Richard to Brel himself. This read:

Dear Breland,

Here is the material we spoke about on the telephone last night. I am not clear why you require it, but I forward it immediately by hand as you requested, on the express understanding that you will treat it as confidential. When you have finished with it, will you please have it delivered to me personally.

With regard to your other question, I can only reiterate what I said on the telephone. Not the slightest unwarranted pressure has been put upon me in connection with this or any other matter.

Sincerely,
Richard Wander.

Typically stuffy, but adequate, thought Brel as Kathleen Taylor came in to the room. 'The Colonel's waiting,' she said.

Brel looked up, irritated by the interruption. 'I know. I saw him downstairs. He's early.'

'Not any more he isn't.'

Quickly Brel shovelled the papers back in to their

envelope. It wasn't fair to keep the Colonel waiting. He suffered from complicated diabetes, and was a sick man.

'Okay, Kathleen. Show him in.'

Brel's last patient that morning was a widow whose ailments were largely psychosomatic, but who preferred a doctor to a priest. She loved to talk, and to some extent permitting her to talk was a kind of therapy. But, glancing surreptitiously at his watch, Brel saw that the hour allotted for his lunch was dwindling rapidly. For once he would have to be abrupt.

Deliberately, he pushed back his chair. 'I'm terribly sorry. I didn't realize the time. I don't want to rush you, but I've an appointment at the London Clinic, a consultation. I really can't keep the specialist waiting.'

Even the widow was not immune to such a broad hint. She rose automatically, still talking. And, as Kathleen had already gone to lunch, it took Brel another five minutes to get rid of her. Then, ignoring the notes he should have been writing up, he ran upstairs to his flat, clutching Sir Richard's envelope.

Over some scrambled eggs and a hastily-concocted salad Brel studied the papers in more detail. Though they formed another link in the chain that added up to another suspect for Chief Superintendent Freeman, by themselves they neither confirmed nor denied Brel's own theory. The evidence, he realized, was entirely circumstantial, theoretical rather than practical, even flimsier than the case against Gerald Hinton. And there was still no apparent motive.

He discarded the advertisements, the references, including the one from the owner of the Gresley Hotel that was heavy on discretion, the correspondence. Perhaps Wander hadn't lied when he'd denied being blackmailed or subjected to pressure. Overt blackmail or pressure, call it what you will, would scarcely have been necessary. Brel wondered if Sally-Ann Belmont had been the only girl that Wander had taken to the Gresley.

He picked up the application form and considered it once again. It was a routine document and contained the usual information. Name, date and place of birth, father's name, mother's name, nationality, education, employment record, names of referees. Thousands of such forms were completed daily all over the country. Brel suspected that only occasionally were the statements in them checked with any rigour. He was laying the form aside when he suddenly remembered a conversation he'd had with Gerald.

Gerald had insisted that no one had any reason to hate him, that he'd never done anyone dirt. As an example of his usual attitude — his good nature, perhaps — he'd somewhat diffidently cited the case of his father's mistress and her child, and his efforts to trace them in the hope of making amends for his father's apparent neglect.

Brel sat, biting the edge of his thumb in excitement as he considered the position. At least there was one fact that could be verified, he thought. Until he'd done that . . .

Some inner alarm forced Brel to the realization that it was nearly two o'clock. Leaving his dirty plates in the sink, he hurried downstairs. In his consulting room, he looked at his appointments book. Tomorrow was a full day, impossible to change. But there was half an hour's gap this afternoon, and with a little rearrangement . . . He found the London Telephone Directory and dialled a number.

'Can you tell me what time you close?' He asked. 'Four-thirty? Fine. And there's no problem if I've got a name and a date of birth? Good.' He put down the receiver as Kathleen Taylor appeared. She spoke first. 'I saw Dr Farre in the hall,' she said. 'He wants to know if you can fit in a patient of Dr Aymer's this afternoon. I said you had a gap, so—'

'I'm sorry, but I can't do it. Tell Farre so. I've got to go out for an hour. In fact, I want you to ring Lady Rowe and ask her if she'd mind coming next week instead of today. Then I'll be free from three-thirty to four-thirty.'

'Suppose she says it's inconvenient?'

'She won't. It's just an annual check, and she only lives in Devonshire Place. Anyway, make an excuse, and another appointment for her.'

'Anything else?'

'Yes.' Brel grinned. 'Stop looking so disapproving, Kathleen.'

'I know what it is,' she said. 'It's those damned murders. I wish you hadn't got yourself so involved, Brel. I'm a bit scared for you.'

Brel laughed. 'No need,' he said. 'no one's going to bump me off.'

For Brel, the next hour and a half were something of a trial. Normally he enjoyed his work, and had a ready sympathy even for his most difficult patients. But that afternoon the first three got rather short shrift, and it was perhaps fortunate that their ailments were minor. It was lucky, too, that the third of them arrived early, so that Brel was free a good fifteen minutes earlier than he expected.

Taking a hasty leave of Kathleen, he collected his car and, for the second time in two days set off for the Aldwych, though not for Doug Brown's place of work. Instead, he intended to visit St Catherine's House at the southern end of the Kingsway, on the Aldwych corner. It was the office of the United Kingdom Registrar-General, and Brel's objective was to trace a birth certificate.

He had never attempted this before in person, and expected to have to fight his way through a certain amount of bureaucratic red tape. In fact, it was all quite simple. Clear notices and amiable porters directed him to a large room crammed with shelves of enormous black and brown volumes, like some Brobdingnagian library. These were the registers — births in one place, marriages in another, deaths over there. A short inspection showed Brel that the volumes were arranged by years and quarters, and alphabetically by name within quarters. There were only two problems. One was the number of people searching busily through the narrow aisles. The second was the sheer size of each book.

Brel identified the book he wanted, but had to wait a little impatiently while a professional-looking character — probably a solicitor's clerk — consulted the volume. However, once the book had been relinquished, and Brel had it firmly planted on part of one of the sloping desks that separated the shelves, he turned the pages and ran his finger down the entries with rising excitement.

He found what he was looking for quite quickly. All the details were there. District and sub-district of registration. Place and date of birth — in this case, a south-eastern borough of London, almost exactly a year before Gerald was born. Name and sex of child — male, as expected. Name of mother — Mary Melinda, and the same surname as the child. Birth registered by the mother ten days after the baby had been born. The only unusual features, which Brel noted with some relief, were the blank spaces under headings for name and address of father, and occupation of father.

Though these gaps were not unexpected, Brel thought he should confirm their exact significance. He consulted a kindly-looking middle-aged woman behind a desk with a large notice 'Enquiries' hanging over it.

'Oh yes,' she said, as soon as Brel had put his question. 'We're asked about that all the time. If the mother registers the birth, she doesn't have to give the father's name. Almost always the child's illegitimate. She may not even know the father's name, or he may be married to someone else, or she could have a lot of reasons.' The enquiry lady looked at Brel speculatively. 'If it worries you, you know you can get a short form of certificate, where there are no spaces to show up these blanks.'

Brel hastened to assure her that he was not personally involved. 'It — it's for a story,' he said weakly.

'Oh yes,' said his informant. Her expression implied that she'd heard that one before.

As he made his escape Brel wondered if he should have ordered a copy of the birth certificate, but the notices inside had told him that this would take a few days to arrive; in any case, the police could readily get one if necessary. For his own purposes, the notes he had taken should be quite adequate.

Walking back to the side street where he had managed to park his car, Brel reviewed his next steps. In fact, they were obvious. First, he must get in touch with Gerald. Then, given the right answer, he could possibly have something to put in front of Chief Superintendent Freeman.

By the time Brel reached Harley Street he was ten minutes late for his four-thirty appointment. Kathleen Taylor was waiting for him impatiently.

'A Sergeant Bill Anderson phoned.'

'What did he want?'

Brel felt hot and sticky and vaguely disquieted. He was uneasy about his conclusions. He went to the hand basin in Kathleen's office and splashed cold water over his face, patted it dry, then washed his hands. He remembered he hadn't yet written up his morning's notes.

'He said he was speaking for Chief Superintendent Freeman. The Chief Superintendent would be most grateful if you'd meet him at the Arts and Letters Club this evening. He'll be there about nine.'

Brel grunted. 'Right. Right. Bring up Mr Porter, will you? I'm ready for him now.' He sat down at his desk and flicked through his notes on James Porter, his next patient. Suspected gall bladder but, as usual, nothing had shown up on the X-Ray. Damn! 'And, Kathleen—'

'Yes.' She was almost out of the door.

'When you've a minute get Gerald Hinton on the phone. He'll either be at home or at his printing plant.'

Kathleen looked at him in exasperation. 'I thought this was meant to be a doctors' practice, not a private detective agency,' she said reprovingly as she swept out of the consulting-room.

Brel grinned at her departing back. She'd got a point, he admitted, and he turned his mind to Mr Porter's problems. Twenty-five minutes later, as he was saying goodbye to his patient, he remembered Gerald.

He buzzed Kathleen on the intercom. 'What about Mr Hinton?' he asked. 'Didn't you get him?'

'He's at his plant, but he wasn't in his office when I called. They'll find him and ask him to phone—' She stopped as the telephone in her room rang. 'That may be him now. Shall I put him through?'

'Please.'

Brel lifted the receiver and waited till he heard Gerald's voice. 'Hello,' he said. 'How are you?'

'I'm fine, Brel,' said Gerald with surprising cheerfulness. 'Just fine. I was going to call you. D'you know what's happened?'

'No, what?'

'Elizabeth phoned. She's coming here tonight.'

'You mean—'

'Yes. Apparently she told her family where they get off, and she's coming here—to me—till the storm's over. That's all she had time to say.'

'Gerald, that's great! Good for her! And congratulations to you both,' Brel said hastily. The minutes were galloping by and he still had two patients to see. 'Gerald, listen. I'm terribly busy and I can't talk for long, but there's something I've got to ask.'

'Yes.'

'It's your father. You remember you told me about his illegitimate son. I know you don't know the woman's surname, but surely the letters were signed in some way. What about her first name?'

'It was Melinda.' The reply came immediately. 'An odd name. I'd never come across it before.'

'And those advertisements you put in the papers when you were trying to trace her. What did they say?'

'They were worded pretty carefully. They said that if anyone called Melinda who had been acquainted with Edward Hinton, or her son, would contact my solicitors, they might hear something to their advantage. Something to that effect. As I said, it's a most unusual name, and I thought it might do the trick. But no. Maybe she's dead and the son's emigrated or something —'

'One more thing, Gerald. You said the son was about your age. Can you be more exact?'

'Sure. It was quite clear from the letters that he was born about a year before me. But why —'

'I can't explain now. I'll call you later tonight, Gerald, or you call me. Goodbye.'

Brel put down his receiver, cutting Gerald off in mid-sentence. This could be it! Here was someone with a potential reason for hating Gerald, if for instance he had come to believe that as Edward Hinton's elder son he should have inherited the estate.

In practice, what might have happened? Melinda's son could have seen one of the advertisements giving his mother's first name. If he were indeed Sally-Ann's murderer, he was a clever and devious man. So, perhaps knowing something of his background, he might have decided to contact the solicitors circumspectly in the first instance—one of Gerald's crooks or cranks maybe. He'd have discovered there was nothing for him directly, and left in anger, determined to revenge himself on his younger half-brother.

This was all very well, thought Brel, but the man would have to be mad, almost certifiably insane, to blame Gerald for his father's sins and, what was more, to plan the deliberate murder of a girl in no way connected with the Hintons merely for revenge on Gerald. Why not take the obvious and decisive step of killing Gerald? Without capital punishment the State wouldn't do it for him, even if Gerald were eventually found guilty of murder. The man in question might be devious, but this was madness.

Brel shook his head, the euphoria of a moment ago quite dissipated. It still didn't make sense. He couldn't really believe he'd reached the right conclusion, that there was not some other explanation.

CHAPTER 17

By seven o'clock that Tuesday evening Brel thought he was finally finished in the office. It was an hour since Kathleen had shown out the last patient, and by now all the neglected paperwork had been completed. He stood up and stretched himself luxuriously. It had been quite a day, he thought, and it wasn't over yet. He still had to meet Chief Superintendent Freeman, and have a serious talk with him. He wondered idly why Freeman had taken the initiative in making a date. Was it possible the police had learnt of his own amateur attempts at investigation?

Brel decided to make himself a quick supper, and then visit a patient on his way to his appointment with Freeman. After his meal he set off, reaching the Arts and

Letters shortly before nine. He parked easily, and took his medical bag into the club with him. There were so many thefts from parked cars that he never liked to leave it unattended.

For once Roberts was not on duty in the hall. Instead it was a porter called Higgins, who was almost a club institution. He was getting on in years, was slightly deaf and known to be lazy and more than a little incompetent. Jenson had tried to sack him more than once, but the older members of the club had always intervened.

'Good evening, sir,' he said. 'You know the dining-room's shut.'

'Yes,' said Brel. 'I thought of that, so I've already eaten. Has Chief Superintendent Freeman arrived yet?'

'The Chief Superintendent?' Higgins frowned. 'No, I don't think so. I haven't seen him.' He broke off. 'Look, there's Mr Jenson. Maybe he'd know, sir.'

'Yes, perhaps. Thanks, Higgins.'

Alan Jenson had come out of the passage leading to the Coffee Room and was moving to the lifts. He paused and waited for Brel to come down the hall towards him. 'Good evening, Dr Breland. You wanted the Chief Superintendent?'

'Yes. I've got an appointment —'

'He's downstairs in the basement. He's been there some time.'

'But Higgins said —'

'Oh, you know what that man's like. He missed him, I expect. I'll take you down myself. You probably don't know your way about our nether regions.'

As Brel hesitated slightly, Jenson pushed the button by the lifts and one set of doors opened immediately. Politely the secretary waved Brel ahead of him, stepped in and put his finger on the square marked 'B'. It was all done so quickly and pleasantly that Brel's misgivings had no time to give way to action. The last thing he saw as the lift doors slid together was Higgins's grey head again bent over his evening paper.

A faint jolt indicated that the lift had stopped. 'Perhaps you'd follow me, Dr Breland,' said the secretary. 'It's a little confusing. At one time all the kitchens were down here, but since we rebuilt them upstairs we only use part of the basement for storage. I can't think what the Chief Superintendent is doing.'

Jenson turned right when he got out of the lift. Brel followed, his anxieties relieved by the total normality of Jenson's behaviour. The way led through what seemed to be a network of stone passages, dimly lit by overhead bulbs, and with doors here and there on either side. From somewhere came the quiet hum of an electric motor. Otherwise the place seemed utterly deserted, as quiet as the grave. Brel suppressed an involuntary shiver.

'Where is Freeman?' he asked loudly.

'Just along here,' Jenson replied. He turned sharply to the left and switched on a light, gesturing for Brel to go ahead. Brel turned the corner and caught a fleeting glimpse of a short passage with a metal door at the end. Then for the second time since he'd met Sally-Ann Belmont, blackness descended.

It was cold, appallingly cold, like a wound that pierced right through the body. That was Brel's first impression as he slowly regained consciousness. And he felt tired, desperately tired, exhausted. He tried to bury back into peaceful forgetfulness, but a part of his brain kept reminding him that this was the one thing he must not do. He started to shiver convulsively, and the involuntary movements helped to bring him back to fuller wakefulness.

He groaned softly as his eyes, their lids heavy, forced themselves open. He found himself staring up at a ceiling of silvery metal — aluminium, perhaps — in the centre of which a small blue light glowed dimly. He lifted his head and at once a sharp pain shot through his temples, so that he winced and cried out.

Without conscious thought Brel began to move his legs, to hug himself, to rub his upper arms. It was freezing. This was a cold that could hurt, that could kill . . .

If only he weren't so tired. Once again Brel opened his eyes and, moving his head very gently, looked about him, this time with a growing sense of horror as he remembered the metal door, and realized where he was.

The club's walk-in freezer was about ten feet by twelve feet, its metal walls lined with shelves. From the ceiling, on long hooks as if in a butcher's shop, hung carcases of meat. In the eerie light of a single blue bulb, they were beginning to look nightmarishly human. Brel gritted his teeth in an attempt to stop them chattering. Everything, he saw, was white with rime and fringed with minute icicles. Even his black medical bag on the floor beside him had lost its leathery sheen and was a dull grey.

Brel looked at his watch. It was just after eleven. He'd been unconscious — and freezing — for about two hours. The freezer was unlikely to be opened till — when? — perhaps sometime between breakfast and lunch the next morning. Brel knew little enough about freezers, but he felt certain that twelve hours in the temperature of this one would be fatal. Quite simply, Jenson had left him here to die.

Slowly and carefully Brel pulled himself upright by hanging on to the shelving. At one point he touched a tray full of lamp chops, and felt his skin begin to freeze to the metal. Cursing, he tore his hand free, leaving a spot of blood behind. There was more blood on the corner of the tray where it jutted over the edge of the shelf, he noticed, and feeling the wound at the side of his head he guessed it was his own blood.

As usual, Alan Jenson — Melinda's son and Gerald's

half-brother—had planned carefully and been very thorough. Brel and his investigations—his snooping—had come to represent a danger, so Brel must be eliminated. But two murders in the club were quite enough; the third death must appear accidental. The sequence was clear: the phoney telephone call ostensibly from Freeman, enticement into the basement—what a fool I was, Brel thought—a blow on the head, the unconscious body dragged through the insulated door, the blood carefully smeared.

Brel could imagine the secretary, his face expressing the deepest concern, talking to the Chief Superintendent the next day. 'A dreadful accident, dreadful. Dr Breland must have gone into the freezer for some reason best known to himself, and slipped and knocked himself out. Of course the room should have been checked before the door was locked, but really the doctor shouldn't have been there at all. I'm afraid that recently he has rather been playing the private detective, you know, questioning the staff, and so on.'

It would all sound very plausible, and there would be some supporting evidence. In any case, there would be little or nothing against Alan Jenson. Higgins's evidence about seeing them together in the hall wasn't really relevant. Even if the old boy had been watching, there was no indicator to show which way the lift had gone; Jenson would merely claim to have dropped Brel off at the drawing-room floor, and gone on up to his own quarters. There would be a post mortem, of course, but it would be hard to demonstrate that the lesions on his head were caused by two blows—one from Peter Dale and one from Jenson—rather than a blow and a fall. The cause of death would clearly be hypothermia, and Jenson had presumably made sure that this was credible. No, it was a very fair bet that Jenson would get away with this—his third murder.

'Not if I can help it,' Brel said aloud, the words issuing from his mouth in puffs of white cloud. By now he was hanging on to a shelf and trying to run on the spot. His head hurt abominably, but he no longer had any overwhelming desire to sleep. He knew he must kept awake and active to have any chance of survival. And he must use his brains.

First he tried the door. It was a wild chance, but it occurred to him that Jenson might not have expected him to regain consciousness; it would be absurd to die if he could just walk out of the place. There was what seemed to be an emergency handle, presumably for use if someone were shut in by mistake, and Brel wrapped a handkerchief around this and pulled and pushed. It was of no avail. The mechanism must have been rendered inoperative in some reasonably explicable fashion.

Angry and frustrated, Brel banged his fist on the door and the wall beside the door. The wall made a considerable and comforting booming sound — it was obviously made of metal plates with insulating material between — but soon he realized he was wasting precious energy. There was no one to hear. The basement was obviously deserted, and there was no chance that old Higgins would be conscientious enough to explore the cellars in the course of the night. Probably Higgins's presence tonight had been part of Jensons's careful plan.

To hell with Higgins, Brel thought. There was no point in pinning one's hopes on a lost cause. He began to inspect and search the freezer thoroughly, in the hope of finding some kind of alarm button. Pulling out trays of meat was an exhausting occupation. They were heavy. The metal froze to his fingers. And he found nothing.

It was depressing, but he didn't despair. He thought of trying to fuse the blue light in the hope of affecting other lights in the club, and bringing someone to seek a source for the trouble. But the bulb was high in the ceiling, and probably on an isolated circuit. In any case there seemed no way of reaching it. Angrily Brel abandoned the idea.

The refrigeration equipment looked a little more promising. High in one wall was a medium-sized fan covered with wire mesh, which seemed to operate intermittently, presumably in accordance with commands from the thermostat. If he could stop it, he could prevent any more icy air being forced into the room, though it would probably not affect the cooling apparatus itself. The temperature in the freezer would scarcely change before morning, but an attempt could do no harm, and an alarm somewhere might indicate a malfunction in the freezer.

Brel yearned for warmth, as if for water in a desert. Instead of concentrating on his immediate problem his mind kept flying off at a tangent. A roaring wood fire. A bath as hot as he could bear. The sun burning his body as he lay on white sand after a swim. Soup, home-made tomato soup, a great bowl of it.

Brel seized a leg of lamb—an excellent club when frozen solid—struggled up the shelves and attacked the mesh covering the fan. This presented little difficulty, and he was soon able to tear it away. The fan itself was a different matter. It was a heavy-duty model, and he failed to do more than dent it, in spite of a hard battering. Eventually, however, he succeeded in jamming the meat into the blades so that the fan was stopped. Ominous noises came from the motor. He could only hope that an alarm would sound.

He could think of nothing else. The exertion had exhausted him. It required a great effort to continue to rub his limbs and do his simple exercises. He knew he wouldn't be able to keep up even this amount of movement for long. And once he stopped, once he relaxed, coma, and eventual death, were inevitable.

He knew that, in spite of the exercise, his pulse rate was

slowing, but he had to rest. Sitting down, he stumbled over his bag. Was there nothing in there that might help him? There were no drugs to treat hypothermia, but perhaps he had something that might keep him active a little longer. Adrenalin — that was it. At least it would stimulate his heart for a while. Its side-effects in the present situation were unpredictable, but they could hardly make matters worse. What was more, the drug was injected subcutaneously, so he wouldn't have to face the almost impossible task of finding a vein.

Brel's hands were shaking as he found a disposable syringe of a suitable size, and he had great difficulty in filing the tip of the glass ampoule with the little metal saw, and breaking the glass. Nevertheless, eventually he prepared the injection. It was a further major effort to shrug off one arm of his jacket and roll up his shirtsleeve. He didn't bother to clean the skin, vaguely remembering studies from his student days proving that swabbing had no significant effect on the infection rate from minor injections. He just stuck the needle under the skin of his upper arm and pressed the plunger. Hurriedly he replaced his jacket. The drug should work quite quickly, but he couldn't wait for it. But now he was buoyed up with a little hope, and though he knew the hope might be spurious he found himself able to begin to jog on the spot again.

Time crawled by. Without the drug and the hope it provided Brel would have given up. His head hurt. He could no longer feel his hands or feet. Slithers of ice formed inside his nostrils. His heart was pumping hard, partly as a result of the injection. Gradually the rests he was forced to permit himself grew longer and longer, and each time it was a greater mental and physical struggle to rise to his feet and start to move. Then he caught himself dozing, and he knew the end must be quite near. There was one more simple thing that he must do. Slowly he made his hand crawl across the cold floor towards his medical bag . . .

CHAPTER 18

Brel opened his eyes and became fully awake. He stared at the plain hygienic furniture, felt the slight pain from the drip in his arm, was aware of the faint smell of antiseptic typical of all hospitals. Suddenly he shivered, remembering Alan Jenson and the freezer at the Arts and Letters Club.

A nurse bustled into the room. 'Ah, Dr Breland, how are you feeling?'

'What—'

'No questions at the moment, Doctor. You're still pretty weak.'

Brel opened his mouth to speak, only to have a thermometer popped into it. He felt the dry firm grip on his wrist as his pulse was taken, and the pressure of the cuff on his arm as the nurse checked his blood pressure. At least he couldn't be too ill; this was no intensive care unit.

He relaxed a little, then tensed again. There was something he had to do, something urgent, but he couldn't remember what. It was connected with Jenson and Gerald, but . . .

He made no move until the nurse took the thermometer from his mouth. Fully aware of the vagaries of hospital routine, he knew it was quicker not to fight it. As soon as he could speak, he said, 'Nurse, what day is it? What time?'

'It's only just after lunch on Wednesday, Doctor. You were brought in early this morning. Now, try to sleep again. You know as well as I do that it's the best thing for you.'

'Maybe. But first get me a telephone, will you?'

'Doctor, there's no need for a phone. If you're thinking of your practice, everything's been arranged. Your partners are aware you're here, and your secretary, Miss Taylor, said she'd look in this evening.'

'Good.' Brel tried to be patient. 'But I must speak to Freeman — Detective Chief Superintendent Freeman of Scotland Yard — right away.'

'That's arranged too, Doctor. There's a constable outside your door who's to call the Chief Superintendent as soon as you can see visitors.'

'Tell him to call now then. It's important, Nurse.' Somehow Brel managed to convey his sense of urgency, and the nurse hurried from the room.

Alone again, Brel tried to think, but he found it hard to concentrate. He began to feel more and more anxious, without being able to pinpoint the cause. But his worry was alleviated a little when the nurse returned with the news that the Superintendent was on his way. Indeed, he arrived, accompanied as usual by Sergeant Anderson, within the next ten minutes.

'Jenson?' Brel said at once, breaking in on Freeman's friendly greetings and enquiries after his health. 'What's the position? Tell me quickly.' He hoped that if he could talk over the events of the previous night he might remember what was nagging at him.

'Officially he's helping us with our enquiries. We'd like to be able to follow your advice and charge him with the murder of Doreen Blunt.'

'Doreen who?'

'Sally-Ann Belmont was just a stage name. She was born Doreen Blunt,' Freeman explained. 'But I don't know if we can make it stick. Jenson denies everything.'

'He can't deny shutting me up in that freezer!'

'He does. He says he was probably the last person you saw, which is why you thought he was responsible.'

'That's a load of rubbish! It's true I don't remember a thing since I passed out in that damned freezer, but—' Brel was beginning to get angry. 'What happened? How was I found?'

'As far as we can make out, it was like this. Roberts found you, probably not very long after you lost consciousness.'

'Roberts? That old boy Higgins was supposed to be on duty; that was part of Jenson's plan. He knew Higgins would never bother to check on the basement.'

'Higgins wasn't feeling well, and Roberts, who's a widower and lives nearby, agreed to come round at midnight and do the rest of Higgins's shift. Incidentally, they didn't tell Jenson what they planned, because the secretary was always looking for excuses to sack Higgins.'

'It's a bit like Dora Brown's salt-free diet,' said Brel.

Chief Superintendent Freeman frowned. He wasn't sure what Brel was talking about, and was given no chance to ask. The nurse had returned and was regarding her patient anxiously.

'He's had enough,' she said firmly. 'He must rest. It's only a few hours since he was being treated for hypothermia.'

'Oh, for God's sake, Nurse,' said Brel. 'I'm the doctor. I shan't rest till I know what's going on. He looked at the drip in his left arm. 'And what about this thing?' he added. 'It's nearly finished. Am I supposed to have another? Or can we dismantle it?'

The nurse looked at him doubtfully, but he smiled at her, and she gave in. 'No, it's the last, Doctor,' she said. 'I'll take it down now. And they can stay a while longer. Maybe it's best if you don't worry.'

As soon as she had finished her ministrations and left the room, Brel said, 'So?'

'There's not a greal deal more, really,' said Freeman. 'You managed to jam a chunk of meat in the works. That didn't make any difference to the temperature—you'd certainly have been a goner if you'd been left till morning—but it was enough to trigger a red light over the freezer-room door. It's an old-fashioned freezer, and there's no alarm upstairs. In any case, Roberts, being a conscientious chap, did check the basement, and saw the light. He knew this meant there was something wrong, so he went and got the keys and found you.'

'And?'

'Well, Roberts dragged you out and you were conscious for a few moments. I gather you said something like, "Don't tell Jenson. Get the police.", and Roberts had enough sense to do as you said. We arrived at the same time as the ambulance, and we found the note you'd written on your prescription pad, accusing Jenson. We weren't greatly surprised.' The Chief Superintendent paused. 'We weren't that far behind you, you know.'

Brel considered this comment in silence, and stared hard at Freeman, who had the grace to look away. Sergeant Anderson was concentrating on a corner of the room.

'What made you suspect Jenson?' asked Freeman finally.

'First, he seemed to me a pretty good candidate for playing that hoax on Gerald Hinton. Only a few people knew when Gerald would be arriving at the club, knew about the stag party, knew that I was a close friend of his who'd be there to confirm Sally-Ann's story that she was pregnant. And, what's more, he knew about the décor—the gold and white decorations—so that Sally-Ann could match them. She spent a lot of time finding that costume, you know. I've got a feeling she and Jenson knew each other quite well, probably at the Gresley Hotel—you know about the Gresley, Chief Superintendent? Jenson used to work there.'

'We've heard of it, yes. But what about the killings?'

'I suppose there were a whole lot of little things — there always are, I imagine. He knew the club well. He could tell Sally-Ann how to get out of the cloakroom by the service door and go up to the third floor. He'd got all the keys — to Gerald's room to plant that ridiculous bag, to the display cabinet with the dagger, even to the ladies' dressing-rooms when he had to hide Dora Brown's body.'

'Dora saw him replacing the dagger, of course,' said Freeman.

'Yes. That was the point of her salt-free diet. She suffered from hypertension and couldn't eat in the staff canteen. So she brought sandwiches, but didn't tell Jenson because she thought he'd be annoyed, and she was there by the cloakroom when she should have been at supper.'

There was a pause while Brel sank back against his pillows. The nurse was right; he was tired, exhausted, but he was still troubled about something he should remember. With Jenson in the hands of the police there could surely be no further danger, yet . . .

'We don't disagree with you, Doctor,' said Freeman. 'I repeat, we'd like to charge him. But the evidence — it's all circumstantial. If we had a credible motive, it might be different — at least we'd have a case to confront him with. But all we've got in the way of motive is — what? — envy, hate, a determination to see his half-brother in prison.' At this, Brel looked up sharply.

Freeman said, 'Yes, we've confirmed the relationship, thanks to your note. How did you get on to it?'

'I don't quite know,' said Brel. He was hesitant to mention Wander, and temporized a little. 'There was so much against Jenson that I decided to check his background. People's backgrounds start with being born, so I went to St Catherine's House. When I saw he'd been registered in his mother's name, the whole thing tied itself up—Gerald's father, his illegitimate son, everything. Luckily Melinda was an odd name, and a call to Gerald clinched the matter.'

'I see,' said Freeman. 'But even so the motive's not strong enough; a case against Jenson would never get to Court.'

'So what you really mean, Chief Superintendent,' said Brel, 'is that Jenson's only got to keep his mouth shut to get away with everything—two murders, an attempted murder and the mud that'll stick to Gerald, not to mention the problem with his engagement. Incidentally, Elizabeth—she's his fiancée—has more sense than Jenson supposed. She left home and went to Gerald yesterday.'

'It's better than that,' said Freeman. 'I gather the wedding's on again. It seems her father accepted the inevitable.'

'That's great news,' said Brel. 'But I'm right, aren't I?'

'About Jenson's position? Yes, that's what it looks like, I'm afraid. On the other hand, what's Jenson really getting out of it?'

Brel was reflecting gloomily how closely Freeman's thoughts paralleled his own, when Sergeant Anderson, who had been silent until now, suddenly intervened. 'It's not right, sir, as we were saying in the car. It's out of character. There's something missing. No one like Jenson would plan anything so carefully and put such effort into it without a concrete reward. If only there was a fortune involved—'

'But there is a fortune involved,' interrupted Brel. 'Gerald's. If only Jenson had tried to kill *him*—'

'How would that help?' asked Freeman.

Brel stared at the Chief Superintendent. 'You mean to say Gerald never mentioned his own damned will?'

'What will?' said Freeman blankly.

'God! He was stupid not to tell you. But I can see why

he wouldn't. It was just a quixotic gesture, and it couldn't have seemed relevant.' Brel went on to explain, concluding, 'I know what you're going to ask—how could Jenson know about the will? The same question occurred to me, and I wondered— Look, let's assume that Jenson was one of those who answered Gerald's ad. In that case, at least he'd be in touch with the solicitors who were handling Gerald's affairs. Isn't there some way he could have capitalized on that—a few words let slip, a drink with a clerk, a chance to look at papers . . . I know it's a bit weak,' Brel finished doubtfully.

'If there's anything in what you say,' said Freeman, 'there should be a record of him at the solicitors.'

Brel thought for a moment. 'Not necessarily,' he replied. 'Suppose Jenson were harbouring a grudge against his unknown father—suppose he was looking for some kind of revenge as well as cash—he would probably have been very careful how he tackled the solicitor. He could have used an alias till he saw how the land lay, for instance.'

'But we still can't see why he should bother with all the elaboration,' objected Freeman. 'Why not just simply kill Gerald?'

'He'd be an obvious suspect when he claimed the inheritance if Gerald had been murdered,' Brel said thoughtfully. 'He'd have to be certain it looked like accident or suicide. Suicide!' Brel sat upright in his excitement. The vague nagging at the back of his mind had ceased. 'That's it! It must be! You know about the phone call to the Dawsons? I've just remembered it.'

'Tell me,' said Freeman resignedly.

Once again Brel explained, adding, 'Would either of you have been surprised to learn that Gerald had killed himself? His wedding's off—or Jenson imagined it would be—he's likely to be tried for murder and probably found guilty, and his closest friends even get a phone call hinting at the possibility of suicide. We've been barking up the wrong tree. There may have been an element of revenge or something in Jenson's motivation. But what he's really been up to is perfectly logical and practical — providing some overwhelming reasons for Gerald's murder to be accepted as suicide.'

Brel paused for a moment to catch his breath.

'Once he's murdered Gerald, in some fashion that's credible as suicide, all Jenson has to do is wait till the whole thing's died down, and the solicitors start their serious enquiries. Then he eventually makes sure he comes to their notice. That could be a year or more away, and he'll long have severed any connection with the club. After all, he would be the true heir, and there'd be no reason for anyone to ask about the details of his past history, once his identity was established.'

There was a long pause, then, 'I suspect you've got something,' said Freeman. 'So the sequence of events —'

'—was something like this,' interrupted Brel. Gerald's father died a year ago. A few months later, after he'd seen the advertisement and realized what was at stake, Jenson applies for the job at the club. There are some indications he made a very special effort to get it. He'd discovered that Gerald was a member, and his intention was to get close to him, study him and make a plan — a good, careful, meticulous plan. As far as he knew, there was no hurry.'

'And then he hears about the engagement,' put in Anderson.

'That's right,' said Brel. 'Once the wedding had taken place, all bets were off. Gerald's will would have been invalidated by his marriage and there was no certainty Jenson would figure in any new will. So Jenson has to think quite quickly, and he made the forthcoming wedding and the stag party the basis of his plan.' Brel stopped, then added suddenly, 'But this means that

Gerald's suicide—murder—is supposed to happen right now, while he's supposed to be in shock about Elizabeth and before he's arrested. Where is Gerald? Is he safe? Why didn't that damned nurse bring me a phone?'

'It's all right, Doctor,' said Freeman soothingly. 'Hinton's been on the phone to us already today, enquiring about you. That's how I knew the wedding was on again.'

'Thank God for that!' said Brel. 'And Jenson's in custody. Can you hold him now?'

'Yes,' said the Chief Superintendent. 'I think we can. There's a lot of detailed legwork to do, but these complicated planners often break down when their plans are played back to them. 'Come on, Sergeant!' Freeman moved towards the door, raising a hand to Brel. 'Get well soon,' he said. 'I'll be in touch. Goodbye for now.'

By the middle of the next afternoon Brel was back in his flat. He had been discharged from hospital with instructions to rest for a few days, but he had never felt more restless. The evening paper was leading with the story that Jenson had been charged, so presumably Freeman had done his work well and successfully. Brel was eager to hear the full account, and had tried phoning Freeman without success.

His front doorbell rang, and with rising hopes he went to answer it. The Chief Superintendent was smiling at him.

Once more Brel interrupted enquiries about his health. 'Jenson?' he said. 'I saw the paper, but tell me—'

'It's all over, Doctor. He's confessed, just as I thought he might. We got the name of Gerald Hinton's solicitor and caught him at his office yesterday. He had a list of replies to the advertisement. Jenson's name wasn't on it—that would have been too much to hope—but the lawyer had a vague memory of an applicant who seemed only interested in the contents of Edward Hinton's will. Of course, the solicitor was pretty cagey, but he did make it clear that the advertisement didn't relate to any direct inheritance. Then he was called away for a few minutes and when he got back the man had gone. What's more, we finally got him to admit that that morning he'd been drafting Gerald's new will, and the notes were on his desk. He was a bit ashamed of that,' Freeman chuckled, 'Especially when he learnt the implications.'

'So what next?' said Brel. 'Did you have an identification parade?'

'No. We thought of it, but the solicitor maintained he'd never be certain. After all, it was quite a while ago, and he only saw the man for fifteen minutes. He says he wouldn't have remembered the incident at all if the chap hadn't disappeared so oddly. No, what we did was confront Jenson with the full story. As I said, he caved in. We've got him all right, Doctor.'

'Have a drink,' said Brel.

'No, thanks, some other time. I've a lot to do. But it was interesting what Jenson said above motive. You were right. It was a kind of combination. He'd never knwn his father's name, but he hated him — apparently old man Hinton never gave Melinda a penny after Jenson was born, in spite of his promises. Then, when Jenson found that a son younger than he was had inherited, and had unbelievably made a will in his favour, the chance was too good to miss. Drag the name of Hinton through the mud, and get a fortune, all at once. What more could he ask for?'

The Chief Superintendent hoisted his bulk out of his chair. 'I must go,' he said, making for the door. Then once again he turned back to Brel. 'Thanks a lot, Doctor,' he said.